NMo

PEANUT'S REVENGE

OTHER NOVELS BY RENAY JACKSON

Oaktown Devil

Shakey's Loose

Turf War

Crackhead

Peanut's *Revenge*

RENAY JACKSON

Frog, Ltd.
Berkeley, California

Published by Frog, Ltd.

Frog, Ltd. books are distributed by
North Atlantic Books
P.O. Box 12327
Berkeley, California 94712

Cover illustrations © 2006 by Ariel Shepard

Cover design by Paula Morrison
Book design by Maxine Ressler

Printed in the United States of America
Distributed to the book trade by Publishers Group West

North Atlantic Books' publications are available through most bookstores. For further information, call 800-337-2665 or visit our website at www.northatlanticbooks.com.

Substantial discounts on bulk quantities are available to corporations, professional associations, and other organizations. For details and discount information, contact our special sales department.

Library of Congress Cataloging-in-Publication Data

Jackson, Renay, 1959–
    Peanut's revenge / by Renay Jackson.
        p. cm.
    ISBN 1-58394-109-6 (pbk.)
    1. African American criminals—Fiction. 2. Oakland (Calif.)—Fiction. 3. Sisters—Fiction. 4. Revenge—Fiction. I. Title.
    PS3610.A3547P43 2006
    813'.6—dc22

                                        2005028922

    1 2 3 4 5 6 7 8 9   DATA 11 10 09 08 07 06

Be Careful:
The toes you step on today
may be connected to the ass
you have to kiss tomorrow!

—*Ghetto Proverb*

AUTHOR'S NOTE

This book is based totally on the writer's imagination. Any similarities to actual events are purely coincidental. Although many of the locations are real, they were used only to make the story believable.

SHOUts to ...

MISS TIMOLYN COBB—ALL OR NOTHING BABY

INDIAH JACKSON—LAST BUT NOT LEAST

ARIANA, JELANI (Stumbler), and AIYANA—THANKS TO
YOUR MOM, NOW I'M KNOWN AS "PAW PAW"

RONA MARECH, JENNIFER BALDWIN, ANGELA HILL, JOHN
GELUARDI—THANKS FOR KEEPING MY NAME IN PRINT

HARRY HARRIS *(OAKLAND TRIBUNE)*—DUDE, YOU'RE A
GENIUS. THANKS FOR ALL THE HELP

DERIN MINOR—I WILL NEVER BE ABLE TO PAY YOU BACK.
THANKS, BRO.

PATSY COBB, PHYLLIS "GAMA" COBB, PEARLIE JAMISON—
DON'T WORRY, SNAPPER IS IN GOOD HANDS

ANYONE I MISSED—GOD KNOWS, THANK YOU ALL

TABLE OF CONTENTS

1
FREE AT LAST

Big Ed sat in the courtroom with his fingers strumming the tabletop as if it were an invisible keyboard. Seated on either side of him were his smug-faced attorneys. This case was open and shut, so they felt as though they were taking candy from a baby.

The prosecution's only eyewitness, Vanessa Harris, was found dead one week earlier in her new digs. She had been placed in the government's witness protection program, which created a new identity along with relocating her far from Oaktown, California, to the suburbs of Norwalk, Connecticut. Knowing that she would not be joining them, the prosecution team had the look of losers written all over their faces.

News reporters lined the packed courtroom, but their video camera crews were denied access due to the fact that this was a high-profile drug case. Graphic artists busily sketched the scene, producing numerous drawings that would be displayed on evening newscasts. The bailiff stood off to the side of the court reporters and spoke.

"All rise, The Honorable Judge Harry J. Stone's court is now in session."

Everyone stood as the judge entered from his chamber and slowly lumbered to his chair. Stepping up to his elevated platform, he surveyed the room before he sat down. Stone was sixty but appeared to be fifteen years older. A small man, he stood five-three, weighed one-twenty, wore bifocals, and sported a head full of thinning white hair.

"You may be seated," said the bailiff.

"First on the docket?" asked the judge, already knowing the answer.

"The State of California versus Edward Jerome Tatum, your honor," said the clerk.

Stone rifled through the huge pile of papers on his desk. He appeared to be searching for something, but it was obvious to all in attendance that his search proved futile. Glancing over his bifocals, which sat on the bridge of his nose, he acknowledged the district attorney, whose hand was in the air.

"Yes, Mr. Abercrombie?" the judge asked.

"Your honor, the prosecution requests a two-week continuance."

"For what reason?"

"Well, sir, due to the fact that our star witness was murdered last week, we need more time in order to gather evidence."

"Seems to me that Ms. Harris was your only eyewitness," the judge said.

"That is correct, sir," Abercrombie scrambled, "but we do have additional leads."

"Mr. Abercrombie," the judge stared at him angrily, "it appears to me that you are not prepared, along with having no case. I cannot allow you to keep this man incarcerated while you attempt to find evidence. Motion denied —Mr. Tatum, you're free to go."

The courtroom erupted, with Big Ed's people acting as if their man had scored a game-winning touchdown. Those on the side of law and order shook their heads in disgust. Reporters dashed for the exits, instructing their video crews to set up on the front steps of the courthouse.

Detectives Johnson and Hernandez slammed their file folders down angrily as Big Ed rose up from his chair, smiling at them. They were prepared to testify against him and had a ton of circumstantial evidence, but without an actual eyewitness, they knew the case was weak. They had hoped the prosecution would somehow produce a miracle.

Big Ed shook hands vigorously with his attorneys then joined his folks, accepting hugs, backslaps, and handshakes. The two weeks he'd spent locked up seemed like an eternity. Now free, he headed out the door to hold court with the media. His massive six-foot-five-inch frame towered over everyone.

"Mr. Tatum, how do you feel?" asked one reporter.

"Do you think the case will go back to trial?" shot another.

"Any comments?" inquired a third.

Flashbulbs lit up the morning sky as Big Ed bulled through the throng of reporters towards his waiting limousine. Stopping on a dime, he waved a hand in the air for silence as microphones were thrust in his face.

"America is beautiful, ain't it?" He laughed at his own question.

"Mr. Tatum. . . ?"

Big Ed ignored all questions, got in the backseat of the limo, and waved as the driver sped off. Leaving the courthouse, they cruised around scenic Lake Merritt and got on the 580 freeway at MacArthur. Their destination was Santa Rita Jail to pick up his personal possessions, money, and jewelry.

A transitional institutional facility, Santa Rita sat right off the 580 freeway on the Pleasanton border. Big Ed was pleased that this would be his last visit to the place. After signing for his belongings, he walked out and got in the limo, pulling his stuff out of the giant paper bag.

His next plan would be to resume his spot as Oaktown's kingpin. While Big Ed was locked up all hell had broken loose, but now that he was free, order would be restored.

The white stretch limo hit 580 heading away from Santa Rita back to Oaktown as Big Ed began sorting out jewelry and counting his cash. He didn't seem to care where they were going because the only thoughts crossing his mind were his children and his empire.

Lifting his cell phone from a zip-lock bag, he pushed the power button. The phone rang immediately, causing

Big Ed to flinch momentarily before regaining his composure.

"Talk to me," he spoke softly.

"It's good to be out, ain't it?"

Big Ed heard laughter at the other end of the line. "What's up, Leroy?" he smiled.

"You da man. Listen dude, I got your Benz with me because you ridin' limo all day."

"Leroy, what you done did?"

"Just threw my little brother the best coming-home party ever. Listen dude, the driver has already been told to brang yo ass here, so enjoy the ride."

"Leroy? . . . Leroy?"

The line went dead so Big Ed pushed the "end" button on his phone and stretched out across the spacious back seat. Exhausted from the anxiety of the trial, Big Ed closed his eyes and took a nap. Twenty minutes later the driver lightly shook him.

"We here already?" Big Ed asked, rubbing his eyes.

"Yes, sir."

Big Ed got out of the car and stretched his massive frame. It felt good to be home. He assumed Leroy must have given the driver directions to his crib and silently wondered what other plans his older brother had in store. Not really caring, he went inside his home to shit, shower, shave, and sleep.

The house was a three-bedroom flat located on the corner of 84th & Olive. Painted beige with brown trim, it had a lawn, security gates in front and back, and bars on the windows. Big Ed marched up the walkway, unlocked the door, and went inside. The driver stood at attention on the side of the limo.

"Hello, Edward." His wife always called him that.

"Hey Shirley, what's up?" he asked.

"Oh, I see they let you out?"

"Yes they did, not that you had anything to do with it."

"I'm sorry, honey," her voice dripped sarcasm, "but I thought your new bitch would play that role."

"I ain't got no new bitch."

"You thought you did until she turned on your ass, then you had her killed."

"I'ont know what you talkin 'bout."

"Yes you do—what you wont anyway?"

"I came to see my kids." He was still calm.

"Well, you'll have to see them later 'cause they're at school."

Shirley sat on the sofa watching soaps as Big Ed looked at her with disgust. Feeling no love, he wondered what he ever saw in her anyway. Besides their two kids, they had nothing else in common.

She wore a flowered house robe, scarf wrapped around her head, and slippers. The fine figure she once possessed was now a distant memory. Big Ed hated the way she'd let her body go to waste, but since all she did was eat, lie down, and watch television, the end result was bound to happen.

"See them later, hell . . . I'll just wait," he said.

"No you won't." She got up. "You're leaving."

"Look Shirley, I've been locked up too long to have to come home to this."

"Edward, this is not your home."

"It is as long as I pay the bills."

"I think you should go." She grabbed the phone.

"Oh, what you gone do? Call the police?"

"If you don't leave, I will."

"You ain't callin nobody."

Big Ed jerked the phone from her hand then ripped the cord from its socket. Shirley attempted to snatch it away but was too slow. With his free hand, Big Ed clutched her throat, slightly lifting her off the floor.

"Oh, now you gone hit me?" she screamed. "Hit me den, muthafucka, an you'll be goin right back where you came from!" He knew she meant it.

"Naw, I ain't gone waste my time on yo fat ass." He shoved her onto the sofa.

Big Ed went into the bedroom and pulled a duffel bag from the closet. Packing whatever he considered important, he stormed back out to find Shirley calmly sitting where he left her. Tears streamed freely down her cheeks.

"Baby, let's make love," she pleaded.

"Not in this lifetime." He walked out, slamming the door.

Shirley followed him out, screaming at the top of her lungs. "You dirty bastard, I hope you rot in hell!"

"Aw fuck you, you fat-ass bitch."

"Ya momma da only bitch ah know!"

"Look, hoe"—Big Ed took a step in her direction—"you leave my momma out of this."

"Come on muthafucka, so I can cut da shit outta you!" She produced a very large butcher knife.

"Go ta hell!"

Big Ed got in the limo and instructed the driver to take him to his mother's house. Deciding it would be best to let Shirley cool off, he figured he'd spend tomorrow with his kids. She stood on the porch staring daggers at her husband as the limo cruised away.

2
MID-WEEK GETAWAY

Melody hated the fact that her wonderful vacation was coming to an end. She and Silky had spent the past four days in Lake Tahoe shopping, gambling, sightseeing, and making passionate love. Realizing that checkout time was less than two hours away, she knew they had to get moving or be charged for another day.

Silky had slept peacefully behind his woman in the spoon position, her naked body pressed snugly into his taut frame. Lightly turning her over now, he climbed on top and mounted.

"Morning, babes." He kissed her cheek.

"Good morning, honey."

She spoke while turning her head away from him so he wouldn't inhale her hot breath. Once she felt his meat plunging into her, she no longer cared. Soft moans escaped her lips, blowing directly up his nostrils, but he didn't seem to mind because he was too busy trying to get his groove on.

Melody was forty, Silky twenty-two, but in bed they were the same age. Silky was experienced in the art of lovemaking well beyond his years. Blasting off a powerful load, he rose out of bed and headed for the restroom. She got up and began packing their suitcases.

Entering the restroom a few minutes later, she joined her man in the shower.

"What would you like for breakfast?" she asked while soaping his back.

"Nothing in particular—what you got in mind?"

"I think the cafe downstairs would be nice."

"That'll work," he responded.

Silky stepped out and toweled off while his woman finished her shower. She joined him in the bedroom and got dressed. Today they wore matching gray jogging suits, tennis shoes, and golf caps.

Scouring the room three times to make sure they were not leaving anything behind, they bounced. Silky left a ten-spot tip on the dresser then toted their luggage to the elevator. Getting off at the third-floor parking level, they headed for "The Black Mongoose," which was what he called his '93 Jeep.

Silky hoisted the cases into the back compartment, pulled the cover over it, and then activated the alarm. Hand in hand, they went back to the elevator, riding silently to the second-floor restaurant.

Slot machines rattled noisily as coins dropped into pans for the lucky winners. Silky and Melody were oblivious to it all as they waited in line to enter the diner. The waitress took them to their table, gave them each a menu, then walked away. Two minutes later she returned.

"Good morning, my name is Michelle and I'll be your server. Would you guys like some coffee?"

"Coffee will be fine," said Silky.

"Decaf for me," Melody answered.

"OK, I'll be back shortly to take your order."

In the blink of an eye she was back with their java. Reaching into the pouches on her smock, Michelle pulled out bottles of ketchup, hot sauce, and Tabasco, knocking them over before lightly setting them in place on the table.

"I'm sorry, clumsy me!" she laughed.

"It's alright," Silky said, "just don't drop my food."

Michelle laughed more than necessary, softly tapping Silky's shoulder while Melody looked on in amusement. Plucking a pencil from behind her ear, Michelle pulled an order tablet from her pouch.

"What would you like?" she asked Melody.

"I'll have the continental breakfast with grapefruit juice."

"And you, sir?"

"Steak and eggs," Silky said.

"How would you like your eggs?"

"Scrambled with cheese."

"Toast, biscuits, or muffins?"

"Wheat toast."

"Hash browns or O'Brien potatoes?"

"Hash browns."

"Anything to drink?"

"Orange juice."

"Excellent. Your food will be ready in a few minutes. If you need anything else just ring." She laughed at her own comment.

"Thank you," Silky responded.

Michelle strutted to the kitchen area, attaching the order slip to a holder lined with several others while Silky's eyes followed her every movement. She wore a very short green skirt, which proudly displayed her tree-trunk thighs. The white blouse and green smock seemed to make her ample bosom appear even larger. Five-feet-six on a hundred-and-thirty-pound frame, Michelle had beautiful features—average-sized lips accented with red lipstick, blue eyes, a round face, and pointy nose. Silky found her attractive.

"Like what you see?" Melody asked, snapping him out of his trance.

"Who? Her?" Silky played dumb. "Hell naw."

"Well, she damn sure likes your ass."

"Why you say that, honey?"

"Silky, I think you know." She was composed.

"Know what?" he whispered, smiling.

"You saw her—dropping shit, laughing when nothing was funny, touching your ass, oh—you do know."

"Baby, all I want is you. Now I can't help it if the Johnson charm draws women like flies on shit. It ain't my fault."

"OK, I'll blame yo momma then."

They both burst out laughing as Michelle walked up with their drinks. Placing them on the table carefully, she leaned over more than was required, giving Silky a fine view of her ample cleavage.

"What's so funny?" she asked, smiling.

"A family joke," answered Silky.

"I think it's great," Michelle stated.

"What's great?" Melody questioned.

"That your son thinks that much of you to take you on a trip to Tahoe."

"Michelle." Melody was cool.

"Yes?"

"Would a mama kiss her son like this?"

Melody leaned across the table and stuck her tongue down Silky's throat. Michelle stood there looking stupid.

"I'm sorry," she said, embarrassed. "It's not that you look old, he just looks so young."

"Looks can be deceiving." Melody licked her lips.

Michelle hurried away from them feeling like an idiot, while Melody laughed heartily. Their meals arrived a few minutes later but Michelle was nowhere to be seen.

"Hi, I'm Stella. Michelle went on break so I'll be your server. Do you need anything else?"

"Mama and me are fine," Silky said elegantly.

"OK, enjoy your food."

Stella headed for another customer while Silky grinned at his woman, who was displaying all thirty-two.

"Oh, now I'm yo momma again," she teased.

"Just eat your rabbit food, gurll!"

Melody smiled lovingly at her man as he devoured his meal. Leaving a five-dollar tip on the table, they walked away arm in arm, stopping to pay the cashier for their breakfast. As they exited, Melody spotted Michelle scooping up the tip.

"Look at her!" she pointed, "She may be embarrassed, but the girl ain't no fool!"

Silky glanced back just in time to see Michelle lifting the five-spot off the table. He laughed so hard that tears welled up in his eyes.

"Girl, you crazy!"

"I might be, but that's a greedy bitch there."

They laughed all the way to the car.

3

BACK ON THE SCENE

The white stretch Lincoln cruised up to Club 99 and parked directly in front. Expensive cars littered the landscape, with valet runners making sure not to put even a nick on any of them while parking. Big Ed's spot had been reserved and marked off with orange cones, which were removed at first sighting of the limousine.

Formerly a social hall, the "Nines" (as it was dubbed) had new owners who sought to turn the joint into a nightclub. If they could get a few more d-boys to rent the place for private parties like the one tonight, they would be on easy street, because word travels fast in the hood.

Located on the corner of Cairo Street and Hegenberger Loop, the club's parking lot was spacious and the building huge. It was painted a burnt orange, and a giant neon sign displayed the name. Big Ed was impressed with his brother's choice.

He got out before the driver had time to open his door and peered around, spotting several familiar rides. All of his folks were present. Out of nowhere, three burly football player types appeared, creating a triangle on either side and behind him.

"Welcome home, boss," said one while surveying the area.

"Thanks, y'all," Big Ed responded cheerfully.

The man trailing had his back to Big Ed, looking for anything suspicious. The two others walked stride for stride with him, but their eyes remained on full alert. All three carried semi-automatic weapons and were dressed in black, blending in with the surroundings.

Big Ed slowly pushed the door open when simultaneously the lights flicked on.

SURPRISE!

The band broke into Kool & the Gang's party tune "Celebration" as flashbulbs from cameras clicked nonstop. Big Ed stood in the doorway momentarily blinded by light, with a broad smile on his face.

He made his way slowly through the crowd of happy faces shaking hands, accepting hugs, and from many of the women, kisses in the mouth. As the lights slowly dimmed, creating a party atmosphere, Leroy stepped in front of his brother, grinning broadly before bear-hugging him.

Big Ed lifted him off the floor as everyone watched the brotherly display of affection with admiration.

"Leroy, you done good, dog," Big Ed crooned.

"Man, it's so good to see you, bro!" Leroy was all teeth.

"Now let me go 'foe you break my ribs, shidd!"

The onlookers roared as Big Ed lightly released the vice grip on his brother. Leroy Tatum was older than Big Ed, but he was a much shorter man. Blessed with the same powerful build, he stood a very short five-nine, weighing a muscular two hundred and ten pounds. Just like his taller brother, Leroy possessed a peanut butter-brown skin complexion and clean-shaven face. Big Ed had built a reputation on being violent and killing you in the blink of an eye, but Leroy was worse because he drank a lot and once the liquor set in, his evil temper stood at attention. He was feared even more than Big Ed.

"Yo dog, you go on and socialize, we'll handle business later. Drink up and be merry!"

"Thanks bro," Big Ed responded as Leroy disappeared.

Big Ed had no intentions of getting drunk so he chose to socialize instead. The club's interior was plush, consisting of a twenty-by-twenty dance floor, elevated stage where the band performed, seating for at least two hundred, and a bar with fifteen stools evenly spaced. The DJ booth, situated next to the stage, was also elevated; and floor-to-ceiling mirrors covered most of the walls. Waitresses were scantily clad in extremely short outfits, which gave the impression they were hired more for sex appeal than skills.

Big Ed continued to accept greetings from well-wishers while making his way through the place. To say he was impressed would be an understatement; he considered this joint the bomb. His mind was already calculating how much income the club could generate by having a cover charge, selling liquor, and renting the space for private parties. He made a mental note to meet the owners.

Deciding to eat, he headed for the buffet table. As he bent over to get a plate, another hand beat him to it.

"Let me fix your meal, honey."

"You think I'm incapable?" he asked.

"Not at all, but since the celebration is in your honor, you should not be working."

"What's your name?" Big Ed asked while admiring her frame.

"My name is Crystal." She handed him his food.

"Thanks for my grub, baby."

"You're more than welcome."

"I have never seen you before, have I?" he asked.

"No, you have not," she laughed.

"Well, make sure I see you again before you go."

"OK."

Crystal walked away holding her plate. She was tall for a female, at least five-eleven, and possessed both style and grace. The strapless red silk dress she wore displayed all of her beautiful curves. Matching red high heels caused her to appear two inches taller, along with accenting a pair of sensuously sculpted legs. A light brown skin tone, pearl white teeth, and mushroom-styled hairdo had Crystal turning heads until she rejoined her three homegirls at a table near the center of the room.

Big Ed stood still, eyes fixated on her delicious-looking booty. The girl was both phine and elegant—he would definitely get to know her better. Smiling to himself, he chose the nearest seat and began eating.

To say he ate in peace would be the understatement of the year because after each bite, someone would come up to say hello or wish him well. Frustrated by the interruptions, he was happy to see Leroy again.

"Man, I see you still ain't lost yo touch," Leroy laughed while copping a seat.

"Bro, you'd thank they'd let me eat first."

"Shidd!" Leroy shouted, "most muthafuckas a be glad somebody welcomin dey ass, but yo ass complainin!" He smiled broadly.

"Yeah, I guess you right, but I ain't most people."

"Niggah, you ain't changed—still the same old grumpy-ass Ed!"

"Who's the girl?"

"What girl?" Leroy answered with a question of his own.

"That honey with the red dress." Big Ed pointed at Crystal.

"Crystal?"

"Yeah, that's her," Ed affirmed.

"I'll tell you 'bout her later, but right now we got business." Leroy turned serious.

"Where da boys at?"

"Dey all waitin fa you—follow me."

Leroy led his brother through an adjoining room, which was half the size of the main club area but just as crowded. A second DJ had the crowd grooving to thumping rap beats, with partygoers displaying their best moves on the tiny dance floor.

Opening a wooden door then stepping aside, Leroy allowed Big Ed to enter first. Leroy closed the door behind his brother then told him, "First door on the right, man."

"Leroy, this place is on hits, bro—who owns it?"

"In time, Eddie, in time," Leroy laughed.

Another difference between the brothers was the way that Big Ed wanted answers immediately while Leroy enjoyed dragging out the drama. Each man considered it a flaw in his brother's character.

The left side of the hallway had three doors marked "office," "custodian," and "storage." At the end of the long carpeted hall was a door labeled "kitchen." Big Ed entered the only door on the right, which was the meeting room.

Seated around a long conference table were all the major players in his drug empire. Although many of the faces were new to their position, they were all longtime trusted members. Big Ed smiled at the sight because everyone was decked out in matching white tuxedos.

"Goddamn," he whistled. "Ah ain't never seen so many sharply dressed niggahs in my life, 'cept at mah weddin!"

The room erupted in laughter, with each man rising up to hug Big Ed as he made his way to the head of the table. Sitting down, he watched as his boys followed suit, then called the meeting to order.

"Fellas, it's good to be home," Big Ed stated, "now let's get down to business. First I have to thank Leroy for the boomin party; dis shit off da hook."

"Thanks, man," Leroy responded meekly, proud of himself.

"Now, I understand Silky tryin ta make a play for my

position. Anybody here thank he gone get it?" With no response Big Ed continued, "Good, 'cause if you believe he gonna run mah shit, you may as well leave right now."

"Boss? How you want us ta handle da niggah?" asked Rodney.

"Kill his ass."

Big Ed pounded the table with the base of his fist for emphasis, causing everything on it to shake. Staring intently into Rodney's eyes, he resumed speaking: "Rod, now ah got you pegged foe his job, so you gone hafta lead the charge."

"His ass is grass," Rodney stated convincingly.

Rodney Gates was a deadly individual who had no qualms about killing, so his statement caused no one to blink an eye. He stood six-one on a solid two-hundred-pound frame. A mouth full of gold stood out every time he spoke, which made his permanent sneer seem even more sinister.

"Good deal Rod, I know you gone handle it, but in order to speed up the process, I'm placing a ten-gee bounty on Silky's ass. Payable to whoever offs him, the competition has no rules, just don't get caught by Five-O."

The price tag for Silky's death brought a deadly silence to the room. To Big Ed, it was the response he desired because he knew strategies were forming in the brains of his boys as he continued speaking.

The turf in question was dubbed Funktown, which happened to be the most violent area in the city. Even though Silky sought control of the entire town, Big Ed knew Silky had Funktown under wraps, so they had to wrest control of that turf back from him. The solution was simple; Silky had to be eliminated.

"Now Rod's in charge of Funktown, Leroy takes over for Skye in central, Damon got the hills, and Muggsy runnin Brookfield. Any questions?"

"Just one," said Leroy.

"What's that, bro?"

"Who you takin home ta-nite?"

"Her name is Crystal," Big Ed deadpanned. "Now let's go have some fun—business starts tomorrow"

The room erupted in laughter. They all knew Crystal. It was also known that she possessed class, didn't do dope, and that Big Ed was out of his league. He thought they were laughing because he would be putting another notch on his belt when in actuality, they laughed because he had no chance of catching Crystal Hayes.

Big Ed stood up and made his way for the door with his posse following suit. As they marched through the auxiliary party room, the dance floor parted like the Red Sea. Big Ed casually strutted over to Crystal's table and took her hand.

"Let's dance," he said.

"Okay." She got up smiling as her friends giggled.

The band was playing Tower of Power's old-school hit, "You're Still A Young Man." Big Ed held her close, inhaling her sweet scent.

"Down on mah kneeeeeees. . . ."

"So . . . tell me about yourself," he asked.

"What would you like to know?"

"Everything."

"Could you be more specific?"

"Where's your man?"

"I'm single."

"Kids?"

"None."

Big Ed spent the entire song shooting luggs in her ear. Crystal was game for the play, answering the easy questions sincerely while deftly evading the tough ones. The more he talked, the harder he became. Crystal felt his manhood pressing on her belly and gripped him tighter.

"Oh, you feel that, huh?"

"Yes."

"Well, that should tell you something."

"Really?"

"Yes," he whispered.

"And what should it tell me?"

"That you'll love it."

"Size isn't everything."

"It's important."

"No it's not, honey—pleasure counts the most."

"Said ahm lovin you, yeah. . . ."

"OK, let me spit dis at you." Big Ed bear-hugged her. "When I was rasslin in high school, they had a saying that a good big man will beat a good little man any day."

"That has nothing to do with sex."

"Yes it does," Big Ed stated convincingly.

"OK, you tell me then."

"What it says, in relation to what I'm talking about, is a good big dick will out-perform a good little dick any day, and until you try, you'll never know."

23

"Maybe not, but I'll say this: A good little dick will be accompanied by a good long tongue, and that, Mr. Tatum, will cancel out your logic!" she laughed.

"Honey," he said, "when you want the truth, call me."

Big Ed handed her his card as he led her off the floor.

4
PARTY TIME

Silky rolled up to the valet at Casino San Pablo only to be informed that the parking lot was full. After being instructed to park across the street in the shopping center, he pulled off. Easing the Mongoose into a stall, he parked. Silky and Melody got out.

They rode the casino's shuttle bus back across the intersection to the club's front door. Silky exited the bus first then held Melody's hand as she stepped down to the pavement. Strutting through the entrance, they walked up to the line and waited.

The casino was packed full of gamblers, many with desperate looks on their mugs. Unlike Reno or Vegas, this casino pitted gamblers against one another instead of everyone trying to beat the house. Each player was required to pay a sitting fee for his or her chair. The house provided dealers and made money from the rights to play, but the game was similar to a neighborhood card party where the winner takes all.

The line slowly inched forward as most people stole glances at the elegant-looking couple waiting to enter. Melody wore a body-hugging gold dress that barely covered her behind. She possessed mouth-watering legs and showed them without shame. Her gold-dyed curl was low to the scalp and blended tastefully with her cocoa-butter complexion. She was forty but didn't look a day over twenty-five. Silky was decked out in a gold Italian suit, matching shoes, shirt, and brim. His finger-waved perm jutted out the side of his hat down to the shoulders, with the bottom portion dyed gold. He appeared much older than his twenty-two years, due to the way he carried himself. Silky Johnson possessed a certain air of royalty. When he entered a room, everyone took notice.

Silky handed the tickets to a smiling attendant who tore off half and returned the remaining portions to him. Walking past the curtain into the concert room, they searched for their table.

The concert room was no more than a makeshift banquet hall converted for the occasion. Up front was a stage with two hundred folding chairs lined up neatly before it. Beyond that were the dining tables, which were small with barely enough elbow room. A comfortable arrangement would have been four chairs to a table, but each table had six, three on either side.

Locating their seats, Silky frowned because Melody's chair was directly across from his own. This meant he would be sitting next to a stranger, and his woman would be too, for that matter. A few minutes later the second couple arrived and took their chairs. An older pair who appeared to be closing in on fifty, they seemed upset with the arrangement also. The guy was seated next to Silky and didn't like the fact that he would spend the show sandwiched between Silky and possibly another man.

"Hey, brother?"

"What's up?" Silky replied.

"How would you feel about swapping seats with my wife?"

"That's a bet," Silky said, "I was just fixing to ask you the same thing."

"Good, it's a done deal."

They shook hands as Silky rose up and went to the other side of the table. He slid into the center seat with Melody on the end. A waitress arrived and placed menus on the table.

"Good evening, my name is Brionna," she said. "Would you like to order a drink before your meal?"

"Yes, we will," said Melody. "I'll have a mimosa and you can fix my man a virgin strawberry daiquiri."

The waitress took orders from the other couple then disappeared. By the time she returned with their drinks, they'd decided on dinner.

"We'll start with some of the appetizers," said Silky. "Bring us a plate of those honey drummettes, an order of sushi, and for the main course I'll have roast beef au jus with garlic mashed potatoes."

"What would you like?" the waitress asked Melody.

"Honey, I'll have the Caesar salad with chicken and almonds."

Brionna took orders from several additional tables before

exiting to the kitchen. As she returned with the appetizers, the third couple arrived. White, young, and dressed nicely, he was handsome and she was phine. They didn't seem to mind the fact that they were seated across from each other.

"Hi everybody, I'm Sophia and this is Joseph. He made me come." She laughed at her own quip.

Sliding into the seat next to Silky, Sophia ordered meals and drinks for both of them as the show began. A duo comedy act opened the show, and Sophia seemed to laugh even before the punch lines were delivered. It soon became obvious to all that she'd had too much to drink. Joseph seemed to be embarrassed by her.

The Temptations took center stage, and the applause was deafening. Even though they were called the Temptation Revue and only had one original member, the show was tight. Silky was a Too Short, 2Pac, Biggie Small fan and felt out of his element amongst all the old geezers but was more than occupied by Sophia's wandering hand.

Excusing herself, Sophia headed for the restroom. When she returned she casually slid Silky a piece of paper under the table. He placed it in his pocket without anyone being the wiser.

The show ended with everyone on their feet giving a standing ovation. Silky and Melody said goodbye to their tablemates, then bounced for the exit.

"Honey, let's gamble," Melody said.

"I have a better idea," he returned.

"OK." She just knew he meant sex.

They walked across the intersection engaged in conversation.

"That was a helluva show," Melody stated.

"Yes, it was." Silky could care less.

"See, I like to do things like that."

"Anything to make you happy, girl."

Silky placed his arm around her shoulder as she snuggled up against him, not caring that they were walking crooked. Getting into the Mongoose, Silky rolled onto I-80 with Oaktown as his destination. "More Bounce To The Ounce" rocked on the radio, with both of their heads bobbing to the dope beat.

Silky took the Edwards turnoff and instead of making a left in the direction of Mountain Boulevard and Melody's crib, he turned right.

"Baby, where we goin?" Melody was surprised.

"You'll see," he smiled.

Erik B. & Rakim's cut "I Ain't No Joke" boomed as Silky headed down Edwards (which changes to 73rd after you cross MacArthur). Once he crossed East 14th, the street name changed again to Hegenberger Road. Melody felt the beginning of a migraine from all the rap shit Silky was playing. She'd attempted to show him that old-school music was really the bomb but realized her plan didn't work. As far as music went, they would never be on the same page. She resigned herself to the fact that they grew up in different eras. The generation gap had won again.

When Silky rolled past the Coliseum and ran into a massive traffic jam, he smiled.

"What's this?" Melody asked before answering her own question. "The Sydeshow?"

"Damn right, baby, now we'll party!" he shouted.

"Baby, I didn't know we were coming here."

29

"Like your surprise, don't you?"

"I need to use the bathroom," she said.

"OK, I'll pull over at the Hyatt Regency."

Silky flowed with traffic, which was traveling at a snail's pace, then pulled into the Hyatt's parking lot. Melody got out and ran to the lobby of the hotel, due to the fact that the three-minute ride took thirty.

A white stretch limousine pulled alongside his hoopty, but Silky paid it no mind. He was busy searching his console for a cassette tape to play. Looking up, his eyes became wide as saucers at the gun barrel trained on his cranium.

He attempted to move, but the force of the bullet to his temple caused blood to splatter over the dashboard and on his clothes. Silky was dead before his head slumped over the steering wheel.

The car lurched forward into another vehicle with the pressure of Silky's weight on the horn. Melody, along with the front desk clerks, ran out of the hotel entrance to see what the commotion was about. She noticed a white limousine at a distance turning into the flow of traffic but paid it no mind because the Mongoose had crashed into a parked car with the engine still running.

Melody shouted for someone to call an ambulance then ran over to check on her man. She hoped he didn't have a heart attack or seizure. Opening the driver-side door, she vomited on the spot. Silky's blood was gushing out from a bullet hole to his temple. It was a sight she would never be able to forget for the rest of her life.

5
CLEAN HIT

People filed out of the Nines and headed for their cars, but most would not be heading home. Their destination was one block away to be part of the "Sydeshow." Big Ed instructed Jason (the limo driver) to park over the hill in an empty lot that was undergoing construction for a hardware store. There, he would enjoy the night's foolishness.

The Sydeshow was to blacks what cruising the strip would be to whites, the one big difference being that at the Sydeshow fools peeled rubber, did doughnuts, got high, shot dice, and more often than not, fist-fought each other over petty disputes.

Even though the location changed each week, there were never any flyers or posters advertising the event. It was all done by word of mouth, with Five-O being the last to know. Sometimes it would be on Foothill, Bancroft, 73rd, or like tonight, Hegenberger Road. The only consistent factor was that the Sydeshow's location was always on the east side, and participants traveled from near and far to display their hooptys. Tonight was no different.

The procession inched along as each driver waited his turn in line to spin doughnuts in the large intersection. Hundreds of revelers stood only a few feet away from the action, creating a circle in the center ring. They did not seem to care that one slip of a steering wheel could result in a major catastrophe with several dead people. Also, the thick clouds of smoke rising up from squealing tires had to have an effect on their lungs.

Cars, trucks, and sport utility vehicles cruised slowly along the strip as Big Ed, Leroy, and Rodney watched with amusement. Most vehicles had fancy rims, booming paint jobs buffed to a sparkle, and loud sound systems blaring out favorite cuts.

There were several contingents cruising in packs, led by the Mustangs, which were dominated by classic models from the sixties. As the Hondas, Chevys, Cadillacs, and Beemers rolled, Big Ed watched with a keen eye on anything fresh that he could use on his Benzo.

The SUVs took center stage, inching along casually, when Leroy spotted a vehicle that looked familiar. Sure enough, just as he thought, Silky Johnson was rolling in the Jeep procession. Nudging his brother inside the limo, Leroy pointed out the Mongoose then told him, "Duck down until that fool passes, then get my money ready."

"Man, that fool got nerves," Big Ed stated.

"Why you say that, bro?" Leroy questioned while hitting his booze.

"'Cause he got to know ah wont his ass."

"Maybe he don't know you out yet."

"How you wanna do this?" Ed asked.

"Let's follow the muthafucka."

"Rod, you drive," Big Ed ordered.

Big Ed leaned forward in the seat directly behind Jason's ear, then whispered, "Man, we need to use the ride for a minute—any damages, I'll pay." He handed Jason a hundred-dollar bill before continuing. "Take a short break at the restaurant and we'll come back to get you in an hour."

"Yes sir." Jason was happy to get the money.

"Oh yeah, we need your hat," Big Ed told him.

Jason got out, handed over his chauffeur's hat to Rod, and marched towards the diner. Rodney put the limo in gear then inched his way through the crowd of people watching the festivities. Silky was five car lengths ahead, which suited Big Ed just fine. Leroy checked his glock to make sure he had bullets and everything was in proper working order. The Mongoose hooked a right on Edgewater Drive.

"Fool must need gas," said Leroy.

"No, he don't," said Big Ed. "He passed the gas station up; that clown's going to the Hyatt."

"Catch dat fool, Rod!" Leroy hollered.

"Man, what you wont me ta do, drive on the side of the road?" Rodney screamed back.

"Hell yeah, if you have to," Leroy returned.

"Man, y'all cool it. We gone get his ass, OK?" Big Ed interrupted.

"Cool," both men responded in unison.

Rodney finally made it to the corner when a thought crossed his mind. "Leroy, let me do it," he said.

"Hell naw, niggah, das mah money."

"Well, let's bofe do it, den split da scrill," Rodney said.

"You crazy, I ain't ghin you nuthin."

"Man, you niggahs cut the fuckin drama!" Big Ed hollered. "I'll pay bofe yaw asses, just get dat muafucka foe it be too late!"

As Rodney pulled into the sparsely filled lot, he tugged the chauffer cap down low on his head. Leroy got out the back then moved gingerly behind the car as it eased up alongside the Mongoose. Silky appeared to be searching for something but did notice the huge vehicle pull next to him.

Casually glancing up, his eyes rested on a gun barrel. His mind immediately gave him three options: drive off, pull in reverse then run the fool over, or use his door as a weapon. Choosing the first play, he shifted gears, but just as the lever made it to drive, a bullet to the temple killed him instantly.

Leroy hopped into the back seat sweating profusely. "Go man!" he screamed.

"Good shit, boyyyy!" Rod proclaimed as he drove off.

"Nice work, bro," Big Ed said as he leaned back.

"We should've offed the bitch too," said Leroy while peering back through the window.

"What bitch?" Big Ed asked.

"That one," Leroy pointed.

Big Ed turned around and saw a scantily clad woman running to Silky's car.

34

"Aw, fuck the bitch, she don't know nothin. That was a clean-ass hit, anyway."

"I guess you right, man," Leroy said as he opened a bottle of cognac.

"Rodney, take us to my ride then we'll pick you up at the restaurant," Big Ed instructed.

"Awight," Rodney said.

After collecting Big Ed's car, the threesome left the limo in the diner's parking lot with the keys in the ignition, hat on the seat, and doors unlocked. Big Ed dropped off Rodney then went home with Leroy; he didn't need the drama from Shirley tonight. Tomorrow he would find a place for himself, but right now he yearned for some much-needed rest.

6

LUCKY STRIKE

Detective Nathan Johnson slowly inspected the murder scene while listening intently to the information provided by the uniformed officer. Bending his massive six-foot-six-inch frame over at the waist, he reached inside the vehicle and shifted the gear into park before shutting off the engine.

Reporters mulled about behind the yellow crime scene tape, which was strategically placed to keep the area free of contamination. Television crews set up shop as the newscasters rehearsed their lines repeatedly.

Johnson had seen it all hundreds of times, but it never got any easier. The hardest part was always informing relatives that a loved one was dead. Lifting the body off the steering wheel, he whistled before calling over his partner.

"Manny, get a look at this."

Manuel Hernandez, who'd unsuccessfully attempted
to locate any eyewitness to the killing, headed in the direction of his partner. They had worked as a team for eight
years, and even though these two didn't always see things
eye to eye, they were highly efficient.

"Damn, amigo!" spewed Manny. "Duane Johnson, better known as Silky."

"Right Manny, and I don't think it's an accident that
he's dead the day Tatum uses his get-out-of-jail card."

"I'll say one thing, the guy doesn't waste time."

"Neither should we. Any witnesses?"

"No."

"There was a girl with him, right?" asked Johnson.

"Yes, you know her from the Eagle nightclub—works
as a bartender."

"Let's have a chat with her, man."

"OK," said Hernandez.

Johnson gave the signal for the coroner's office staff to
haul off the body, which they acknowledged and began
their gruesome task. The two detectives walked over to a
patrol unit where Melody sat patiently in the back seat.
Before they reached her, reporters bombarded them with
questions. Johnson silenced them with a hand gesture
then gave a brief statement.

"Ladies and gentlemen, at this time we don't have any
information because our investigation has just begun.
When we do learn something pertinent and all the facts
are in, you will be notified. Now if you'll excuse me. . . ."

"Detective Johnson, can you give us the victim's name?"
asked one newsman.

"Not until the family has been notified and a positive identification has been made. If you will excuse me ..."

"Is it true that there were drugs in the vehicle?"

Johnson bulled past the throng of cameras and headed for the squad car. Hernandez was right at his side, opening the door for Melody to get out.

"Hello, I'm Sergeant Johnson and this is my partner Hernandez. We've met before, right?"

"Yes, we have," Melody answered.

"Your name is...?"

"Melody Boudreaux."

"Melody, what did you see?"

"Nothing." She wiped away a tear. "I went in the hotel to use the restroom and when I finished, we heard a loud commotion, so me and the desk clerk ran out, but he was already dead." Her voice was barely audible.

"How long were you inside the hotel?"

"Couldn't have been more than five minutes."

"Did you notice anyone following you?" Johnson pressed.

"No."

"Anyone pulling out of the lot?"

"Only a white limousine," she remembered.

"OK, we'll have someone take you home. Here's my card—if you think of anything, call me."

"I've called my sister so I don't need a ride, but thanks for the offer," she said.

Melody stepped out of the patrol car, ignoring Hernandez's greedy eyes devouring her statuesque physique. She walked over to the hotel entrance and waited for her sister. Johnson and Hernandez began their usual routine of digging for evidence. They knew that unlike television, in real-life murders somebody, somewhere, saw something.

"Manny, I'll take the gas station; you take the hotel restaurant."

Each man headed in opposite directions. The restaurant was located right in front of the parking lot. The gas station sat on the corner of Hegenberger Road and Edgewater Drive with the lot behind it. After about ten minutes the two detectives met up at Silky's ride, which was about to be towed to police headquarters as evidence.

"I got nothing, Mann—what about you?"

"An elderly couple seated in a window booth were the only customers around the time of the shooting. I have their room number."

"Good work, man, let's go pay them a visit."

Strolling through the courtyard past the swimming pool, Johnson and Hernandez located room 124 and knocked on the door. They heard shuffling then saw the curtain move. Johnson flashed his badge and a second later, the door opened up.

"Good evening, officer, may I help you?"

"Yes, I'm Sergeant Johnson and this is my partner Sergeant Hernandez. May we come inside?"

"Sure, sure."

The gentleman stepped to the side, allowing both men entrance to his room. He was at least seventy years old with thinning white hair, shrunken face, and frail body. Fully dressed in beige cotton dockers, penny loafers, and button-down shirt, he appeared to be dapper.

His wife entered from the bathroom wearing a pink houserobe. She seemed to be not a day over sixty and was beautiful for her age.

"Samantha, these officers have a few questions they'd like to ask us," the old man said.

"My dear," she clutched her robe, "how can we help?"

"Ma'am, I'm Sergeant Johnson and my partner's name is Sergeant Hernandez."

"We're the Montagues, I'm Samantha and my husband's name is Jonathan," she said, extending her hand.

"We apologize for disturbing you at such a late hour so I'll get right to the point," Johnson began. "There was a shooting tonight in the parking lot and we think it may have occurred while you were dining."

"Oh no!" Samantha showed concern. "Was anyone hurt?"

"Yes, there was a fatality." The room was silent.

"How can we help?" she asked.

"Can you tell us if you noticed any suspicious activity?"

"Well no, not really...." She seemed to be searching her memory.

"Did you see anyone or any vehicle?"

"No officer, the lot was fairly empty." She spoke for the both of them.

"Well, here's my card—if you should remember anything don't hesitate to call me."

"There was one car I remember," she said suddenly. "It was a white limousine. I'm not sure if that'll help, but I do remember seeing it drop off a passenger. It happened while Jonathan paid for our dinner."

"Can you tell me the make?"

"No, I can't, they all look alike to me."

"Was the passenger male or female?'

"He was a man."

"What race was he?" Johnson was soothing with his questions.

"My my, it was so dark." She clutched her robe tighter. "I think he was black; I'm sure of it."

"Did you notice where he went?"

"No, because we left the diner and came here."

"Once again, we apologize for the inconvenience and thanks for the information."

"Sorry we couldn't be of much help," she said while shaking their hands.

"You've been more than helpful. If you don't mind, could you give my partner your full names, address, and phone number?" Johnson requested.

"Sure," said Samantha.

Once Hernandez jotted down their information, the detectives walked out into the cool night air discussing their first lead. Maybe it was solid, maybe not, but they now had a trail.

"What do you think, Manny?"

"Never know, Nate, could've been one of those rap guys. You know they always be ... how you say, livin large."

Johnson stiffened at his partner's remark because any chance Manny got, he stereotyped blacks. It always struck a nerve with Johnson, and he felt that sooner or later he would call his partner on it. He also knew that when he did, things would never be the same. Walking quietly to the car, Johnson got in and started the engine.

"You hungry?" he asked through clenched teeth.

"Yeah, I could use a bite," Hernandez answered.

"And get rounder than you already are, you short-ass runt," Johnson thought to himself, then laughed before speaking out loud. "How about something different?"

"What's wrong with the usual spot?" Hernandez inquired.

"Well, since we're out here on the east side, we may as well find a place this way because when we get back downtown, I'm going home."

"OK amigo, you choose," Hernandez said dryly. Normally they ate at Mexicali Rose, which was located one block from headquarters. However, every blue moon they would dine at another spot. Manny never really enjoyed anywhere else but didn't want to rock Nate's boat.

Johnson shifted into drive and hit Hegenberger. The Sydeshow was basically over, but a few riff-raffs remained scattered along the strip. Cruising through the intersection, Johnson hooked a quick left then turned into a Denny's restaurant. As he did so, both detectives' eyes became large as saucers.

"Whatayaknow amigo, a fucking limo, and white at that."

"Manny, it looks like our night."

"You damn skippy it's our night!" Hernandez laughed loudly. Upon seeing the car and realizing that they might not have to go through the tedious process of tracking it down, he was beside himself with glee.

"Nate, you wait right here, I'll check it out."

"Alright Manny."

Hernandez bounced from the car and went to inspect the limousine. Seeing the keys in the ignition, he tried the door handle. Johnson radioed for backup and watched as his partner opened the door and retrieved something. Hernandez returned grinning broadly.

"What you got, man?" Johnson asked.

"A set of keys." He jingled them. "Now why would a driver leave his doors unlocked with the keys in the ignition, a fucking limousine at that?"

"We'll have to ask him the answer."

Nate pointed at Jason, who was heading towards the limo. Finding the doors locked, he stomped violently on the ground, throwing his hands in the air.

"Let's go ask him a few questions," Johnson said, getting out of the car.

Both men approached Jason but from different angles. He saw Johnson but had no idea Hernandez was behind him.

"Excuse me, I'd like a word with you." Johnson flashed his badge.

"You gonna help me get in the car?"

"No sir, I need to understand how you managed to become locked out."

"I don't know, officer, I guess I dropped the keys inside by accident."

"Oh really?" Johnson arched his brow. "So you did lock the door?"

"Yes sir, I always lock the door."

"Did you lock the door using your key or by the door lock switch?"

"The switch," Jason lied.

"How long were you in the restaurant?"

"About an hour—why?"

"And you're certain you locked the door?"

"Pretty much so—you mind telling me why all the questions?" Jason appeared irritated now.

"Because"—Manny interrupted, jingling the keys—"if you locked the door, explain why I have your keys."

Jason, spooked by Hernandez' sudden appearance, quickly regained his composure and said, "I don't have the slightest idea."

Two squad cars pulled into the lot. The patrol officers hopped out clutching their nightsticks.

"What's this all about?" Jason demanded.

"You'll have to come down to the station, sir," Johnson said.

"What if I refuse?"

"Then we'll arrest you," Hernandez stated point-blank.

A small crowd gathered looking on with curiosity.

"Arrest me for what?"

"Suspicion of murder." Hernandez toyed with the key ring.

"Murder? I didn't kill anyone—besides, I have witnesses who will verify that I've been here!"

"Sir," Johnson whispered, "just come downtown, answer a few questions, and if you're clean, you'll be free to go."

"OK," Jason sighed, "let's get it over with."

Hernandez conducted a pat-down search on Jason then

slapped on a pair of cuffs before escorting him to their service vehicle. His partner instructed the beat cops to have the limo dusted for prints then towed to the station. Joining them in the car, Johnson took the 880 freeway to headquarters.

Once there, they locked Jason in an interrogation room then headed for Silky's mother's house to give her the bad news. Johnson hated this task more than any other in police work because family never understood why their loved one was murdered.

A DAY SHE'D
NEVER FORGET

Big Ed arose at the crack of dawn, gathered his things, freshened up, and walked out of his brother's crib. He was happy to go because the desired rest he yearned for was denied due to the fact that Leroy lived in a run-down housing project on Sunnyside.

Street-level dealers sold their poison all night long. Add in dopefiends arguing loudly about any and everything, fools peeling rubber in their hooptys, and rap music blaring from sound systems, and Ed found himself wondering how Leroy ever got any sleep.

Walking slowly to his Benz, he felt his cell phone vibrate on his belt clip.

"Talk to me."

"Is that the way you answer a call?"

"Usually."

"Interesting . . . do you know who you're talking to?"

"Yes," he said.

"I hope I didn't call too early."

"It's never too early for you, baby."

"You're crazy," she laughed.

"Only about you girl," he deadpanned.

"Anyway," she regained her composure, "I was wondering if you were free today."

"For you? Hell yeah, what you got planned?"

"A wedding."

"A wedding? Honey, don't you think we should get to know each other first?"

"Not us, silly!" She laughed louder than the first time. "My friend Chantay is getting married today and I'd like you to be my date."

"What time?"

"One o'clock."

"What color are you wearing?"

"Sky blue."

"What's your address?"

"You're direct, aren't you?"

"You answered my question with one, but you still didn't tell me what I want to know."

"I'm sorry, love, but the only man I know as blunt as you are is my dad."

"Well then, I know he's a great man."

"Yes, he is. I live in San Leandro, a condominium complex called the Parkside Terrace."

"Is that the one by the BART station?"

"Yes, it is." She was surprised.

"What's your number?"

"152, but you have to dial 143 on the front phone."

"OK," he said, "I'll be there at noon."

"Good, I'll see you then."

"May I ask you a question?"

"Now why do I feel that no matter what my answer is, you'll ask anyway?" she said.

"How did you decide on me?"

"To be truthful, my sister was supposed to go with me but she's stressing over her man."

"It's a date, baby."

"See you at noon."

"Later," he said.

"Bye bye."

Crystal rolled over in her bed and pondered what she was getting into. She didn't know Big Ed at all but would rather have an escort than attend the wedding alone. Besides, there's no better way to find out if a new man has a woman than to get him out in public. Smiling at the thought, she rolled back over and dozed off.

Big Ed walked around his Mercedes to inspect the body. He knew no one would mess with it because everyone on the street was aware of who owned that car. However, it was always his custom to walk around his ride looking for any damage.

The block was deserted except for the few drug pushers lurking in the shadows of apartment complexes. Another hour or so and they too would be heading home with phat bankrolls. As Big Ed drove off he waved or honked his horn at each one because they all bought product from Leroy, which meant they were his boyz.

Riding up 98th, he took the 580 freeway to Hayward. Exiting at Foothill, he cruised down the thoroughfare then hooked a U-turn into the parking lot of a pancake house. Since it was still early morning, the eatery was sparsely populated. He was immediately seated.

Big Ed ordered then went outside to buy a paper from the rack. As he waited for his breakfast, he read about himself on page one. The article in question portrayed him as a monster. Disgusted, he tossed that section and read the sports page.

The few customers in the place were reading the same story. Noticing the facial and physical resemblance of Big Ed to the article, they stole glances at him. Big Ed ignored them all.

When his meal came he wolfed it down quickly. The amount of food was enough to feed two people, but for him it would be just right. He had several strips of bacon, link sausages, eggs, toast, hash browns, three giant pancakes, and a pitcher of orange juice.

Stuffed and satisfied, he left a five-spot tip, paid the cashier, and walked out. His original plan was to go to his parents' home in Hayward because he kept a mini wardrobe there. However, while eating he decided to get all of his fine threads from Vanessa's crib.

Big Ed knew this could spell trouble since Vanessa (the woman who could bear witness against him) was dead and the police felt certain he was behind it. If they had the place under surveillance, he would be caught red-handed. Regardless, he'd spent too much money on those clothes to leave them.

Pulling into the Hamilton Park condo complex on Golf Links Road, Big Ed parked in an unoccupied stall, killed the engine, and surveyed the scene. Yellow police tape criss-crossed the door with a red warning notice prohibiting anyone to enter.

Big Ed gently removed the tape and used his key to enter the unit. Nothing happened when he flipped the light switch due to the power being shut off. It was both damp and cold inside. Feeling his way to the entertainment center, he located a candle.

Lighting it, he followed the flickering flame into the bedroom where he retrieved a duffel bag. Placing the candle jar on the dresser, Big Ed grabbed all of his suits from the closet rack then stuffed the bag with shoes, socks, underwear, and hygiene products. Next, he searched for his shoebox full of cash but came up empty.

"Damn police got mah muthafuckin scrill," he said to himself.

Hoisting up his suits and bag, he bounced. First he opened the door for some light then blew out the candle and returned it to its original spot. After closing the door he replaced the tape carefully, then went down the stairs to his ride.

There was a four-hour time gap until he was due to pick up Crystal, so he drove to Shirley's, his former home. He hoped to spend a few hours with his children. Pulling into the driveway he noticed that her car was gone. His next-door neighbor Sidney, who'd been watering his lawn, ambled up the walkway.

"Big Ed, it's good to see you, man." They embraced.

"Yo Sid, you thought mah ass was grass, huh?"

"Man, ah sho did."

Sidney Davis could best be described as a "happy" drunk. He worked a regular job, provided for his family, made extra change by maintaining his neighbor's lawns and doing other odd jobs, and kept his mouth shut. Always in need of a haircut and shave, he posed no threat. Once his workday was over, "Sid" drank until he went to bed. Unlike most people who developed a change in personality while intoxicated, Sid became mellower by the minute. He'd just sit with a stupid little grin on his face, enjoying his world.

"Looks like Shirley ain't here." Big Ed's question was more of a statement.

"Man, you didn't know?" Sid asked.

"Didn't know what?"

"She took a gangload of kids to Marine World—dey left early dis moanin."

"Oh, I see." Big Ed stroked his chin. "Well, dude, I gotta go change clothes, then get busy."

"Awight, Big Ed." They shook hands. "Man, you know ah would'a kept up yo grass but Shirley said she cain't pay me no moe."

"Here Sid," Big Ed slid him a fifty, "that'll hold you for a month."

"Right on, dog."

Sidney hurried to his garage to get his mower while Big Ed grabbed his belongings from the back seat of his ride. Stepping up to the door he inserted his key. Nothing happened; the key would not open it. Surveying the key ring to make sure he hadn't tried the wrong one, he inserted it again. Same result.

"Damn hoe!" he cursed, "done had the locks changed, bitch."

Angrily tossing his clothes back into the car, he drove off. Sidney watched Big Ed drive away with a curious look on his mug. Since it wasn't any of his business, he would do as always and keep his mouth shut.

Big Ed parked in the BART station parking lot, stuffed his wardrobe minus the blue suit and duffel bag in the trunk, then walked across the street to the Parkside Terrace's entry door. Dialing 143 on the security phone, he waited.

"Hello?"

"Hey girl, it's me, hit the buzzer."

"You're three hours early."

"I know, I'll tell you about it when you let me in."

She paused for a minute before speaking. "OK." She buzzed him in.

Strolling through the circular courtyard, Big Ed figured Crystal was still in bed. He peeped out the swimming pool, hot tub, weight room, and social hall before entering a door leading to the hallway. Stopping at unit 152, he knocked. Crystal opened the door wearing a purple housecoat, the thick fluffy kind made out of terry cloth.

"Good morning," he said.

"Hi." She stepped aside to let him in. "Why are you so early?" she asked while closing the door.

"It's a long story."

"Three hours is enough time to tell it."

"OK—let me take a shower first, I feel dirty."

"Follow me."

Crystal headed for the bathroom while Big Ed placed his suit on the sofa and bag on the floor. He accepted the towels she gave him from the linen closet then watched with lust as she bent over to turn on the water. With her back to him, Big Ed began undressing.

"Honey, you have what I call natural beauty."

"Oh really." She flipped the shower switch.

"Yes—I mean you just woke up and still look good."

"Thank you," she blushed. "You'll have to set the temperature to your liking, OK?"

"That'll work."

Crystal turned around, only to face a butt-naked man. Surprised by his bold action, she was rendered speechless by his physique. Rushing out past him, she closed the bathroom door. Her heart raced a mile a minute.

Big Ed's penis was larger than any she'd ever seen—it was so big it scared her. Try as she might, she couldn't eliminate the sight from her brain. Instantly her panties were soaking wet. All she could think about was how good that dick would feel inside her body. She also felt that it might be too big.

Big Ed smiled to himself as he stepped into the shower. He knew the effect his dick had on women and loved to prove wrong those like Crystal who state that "size doesn't matter." She was probably dreaming about it right now. After he turned the water off and began drying himself, the door opened.

"You need anything?" she asked, eyes fixed on his meat.

"Just a little rest, baby—where's your bedroom?"

"It's right here," she pointed.

"I'll take a nap—wake me up when it's time."

"OK."

Big Ed slid under the covers of her king-sized bed while Crystal took a shower. The lavender satin sheets were still warm from her body heat so he stretched out and closed his eyes. Crystal finished her bath, brushed her teeth, then joined him wearing only a skimpy negligee.

Snuggling up behind him, she rested her hands on his massive chest. Big Ed rolled over, allowing his penis to press up against her leg.

"Now why are you so early?" she asked.

"I went to visit my kids but their crazy mama took them to Marine World, so since I didn't have anything to do, I came here."

"You're telling me you don't have a place of your own?"

"That was my place up until two months ago."

"What happened?"

"The bitch wanted to control me, and that just ain't gonna happen."

"What bitch?"

"My soon to be ex-wife."

"You're married!" She sat up.

"Separated, soon to be divorced." He eased her back down. "I'm as single as you are."

"How do you know I'm single?"

"Because if you wasn't, you wouldn't have me in your bed."

Crystal lay silent, wondering what was happening. Big

Ed, sensing confusion in her brain, lightly turned her body to his.

"Baby, I ain't got no woman, but I'm here because I think you're the one for me."

"Oh you do, do ya?"

"Yes I do." He placed her hand on his swollen pole.

Crystal began rubbing it as Big Ed toyed with her clitty. Closing her eyes, she eagerly returned the sensuous kiss he planted in her mouth. As his thick finger plunged in her hole, she gyrated her hips to match his rhythm.

Once he felt she was ready, Big Ed got on top and penetrated. Her cunt gripped his lethal weapon like a catcher's mitt would a baseball. Crystal's eyes rolled to the back of her head and her face displayed a giant smile.

Big Ed caught a rhythm and began slamming his meat into her body with force. Crystal was happily chanting his name, celebrating how good he felt inside her, and repeatedly moaning, "It's so big."

By the time Big Ed placed his giant hands under her ass, elevating her hips off the bed, she was screaming with each thrust. She opened her eyes to look at him but that only seemed to make him thrust harder. He was fucking her eyes shut.

Waves of pleasure vibrated through her body as Big Ed had his way. Blasting off a powerful load of cream, he rose up and went to the bathroom to wash off. When he returned, her legs were shaking uncontrollably. Big Ed smiled and rejoined her under the sheets.

"You like that?" he asked.

"Yes," she panted.

"So . . . you say size doesn't matter, huh?"

"Well, what I meant . . . OK, you were right, it is important!"

Big Ed laughed loudly then rolled her over and took her doggie style. Before their love-making session was over, he'd taken her four times, had Chinese food delivered, made more love, and spent the night. They never did attend the wedding, but Crystal could care less. She would always remember this day as being the best of her life.

8
WORD IS OUT

"That motherfuckin Big Ed, I'mo kill his ass!" Junebug yelled. "The niggah did it an he gone pay!"

"Calm down, Bug," Melody reasoned.

"Fuck dat—dat niggah gone pay!"

Anthony "Junebug" Grimes grieved his road dog's death harder than anyone else. He and Silky were ace-coom-boom since elementary. A playboy, sharp dresser, and ladies' man just like his fallen compadre, he now felt alone.

The home of Silky's mother, Irma Johnson, overflowed with mourners, many of whom disregarded Junebug's threats as just letting off steam. Everyone knew Big Ed Tatum. They also knew that the threats made by Junebug would be relayed to Big Ed.

Junebug knew the word would reach Big Ed too, but he could care less. Strutting around like a gangsta, he had to appear fearless. He was six-foot-one and weighed a solid one-ninety-five. Considered a pretty boy because of his gorgeous high yellow complexion, finger-waved perm, and thick jet-black sideburns down to the jawbone, Junebug and his words just didn't carry the dangerous threat that an ugly man would. He didn't look the part.

Irma's dining room table was piled with food, but most people in attendance chose to drink instead. Liquor was plentiful, with guests not only bringing dishes but bottles too. Being a heavy drinker, Junebug was sloppy drunk, which caused him to resemble a Mexican more than a high-yellow black man.

"Come on, Bug, let me help you to the bedroom—you need to take a nap," said Irma.

"Mama Erm, I'ont need no nap," he whined.

"Yes, you do," she said as she escorted him to Silky's old room.

Junebug sat on Silky's bed and began examining each framed picture of his partner one at a time. His mug was prominently displayed on many of them, which caused tears to roll freely down his face. He cried like a baby, and all Irma could do was pat his back and tell him everything would be alright.

"You know, Junebug, Duane was my only son but I feel like you're my son too," she said, turning even more serious. "Baby, now I know you seek revenge but let the law take care of that."

"Mama Erm," Junebug dried his eyes, "the law moves too slow. Big Ed gone pay and you can count on it."

Irma knew that a man convinced against his will would

be of the same opinion still, so she just hugged Junebug then walked out of the room. Ten minutes later he was snoring loudly.

After a few hours many of the guests began leaving. Melody was busy helping Irma clean up the place when Junebug staggered into the room with his woman "Peaches." She had taken up refuge on the bed with her man. The last of the mourners filed out, leaving only the foursome.

"Mama Erm, you need me to help with anything or to spend the night?"

"Naw baby, I wish to be alone," she answered while gazing at a picture of Silky from prom night. "You guys go on home, and honey"—she spoke to Peaches—"you take care of him, OK?"

"Yes ma'am," Peaches responded, giving Irma and Melody hugs. "Bug, give me the keys," she told her man.

"Junebug, you take it easy and get some rest," Irma said before hugging him tightly.

"I will, Mama Erm; see you later, Melody!"

"Bye bye, Bug," Melody said.

Melody and Irma watched Junebug stagger down the steps to the car. As Peaches let him in the passenger side Melody wondered to herself how he could be so certain that Big Ed was behind it. First chance she got, she would get with Bug and have him explain his logic.

Peaches sped off and headed to her apartment complex, which was located on Foothill Boulevard sandwiched between 36th & Harrington. "Skirbville," as it was called, sat right next door to Ed Howard's Place, a nightclub known for its battle-of-the-bands contests. Next to that was a truck and van rental agency.

Controlled by the High Street Bank Boys, who were an extension of Big Ed's eastside empire, this housing authority complex consisted of welfare mothers. Its design had many flaws with the first being its ugly appearance. A reverse "L"-shaped disaster, Skirbville had three floors, twenty-one units, and a parking lot for eight cars. There was a drive-in entrance off Foothill that served as the only way in or out.

D-boys casually blended in with party-goers and watched with more than a passing interest as Peaches pulled into the lot. Word was already on the street that Big Ed wanted Junebug, so cell phones were put to use pronto. They all wanted that easy money.

"Peaches, come here for a minute," said Fat Daddy.

"What you wont, man?" she said as she struggled to get Junebug out of the car.

"I just need to ask you a question," he answered.

Fat Daddy was the ruler of Skirbville and his features fit the title, which he wore like a badge of honor. Five-six on a portly two-hundred-and-twenty-pound frame, he was black as tar and had a bad habit of rubbing his over-sized belly.

Peaches closed the car door and walked over to Fat Daddy to see what was so important. The hip-hugging black dress she wore displayed all of her assets. Her mug was nothing to write home about, but her body demanded multiple letters. She was stacked.

"What you wont, Fat Daddy?" Her hand rested on her

hip and her posture resembled a prostitute's. "I'm in a rush."

"I just thought maybe once you put that loser to bed, we could party." He produced a hand full of base rocks.

Being a closet dope fiend and itching to get high after all the day's drama, Peaches stared at the rocks while contemplating her next move.

"OK, honey," she was syrupy, "get some of your boys to help me carry Junebug in the house and I'll party with you."

Peaches had no intentions of getting with Fat Daddy's sloppy ass because one, he could not satisfy her, and two, Junebug supplied her with more than enough dope. What she didn't know was that Fat Daddy had no intentions of getting with her either; he had money on the mind—to be specific, the reward Big Ed had placed on Junebug's capture.

"Dave, Troy, yaw help me carry dis fool in da house," Fat Daddy ordered.

The foursome headed for the car with Fat Daddy's henchmen carrying Junebug up the steps to Peaches' second-story flat. All the while he tried to feel under her dress but she slapped his hand away each time.

"Cut it out, Fat Daddy—shit!" Peaches hollered.

"Oh, it's like dat, huh?" he questioned.

"Like what?" she frowned.

"Like you never sayin 'cut it out' when you need dope. Ah ain't forgot all dose times you sucked mah dick fa a hit."

"Everybody makes at least one mistake."

"What?" he got loud.

"Look dude, I have a headache so I won't be needing to get high—you guys can just leave."

Dave and Troy walked out of the bedroom where they had dumped Junebug just in time to see Fat Daddy fire a vicious right to Peaches' jaw. Before she had time to recover, he kicked her in the ribs.

"Bitch, who you thank you talkin to? Ah whup yo mutha-fuckin ass, shiddd. . . ."

"Niggah . . . you gone get yours!" she threatened through clenched teeth.

"What?"

He faked another kick, to which Peaches covered up in a fetal position. Laughing at her defense, Fat Daddy spoke to his flunkeys.

"Man, yaw wont some pussy?"

Before they could respond Rodney and Leroy entered the crib, and they weren't smiling.

"Whatup Fat Daddy?" greeted Leroy.

"Leroy, Rod, how yaw be?" Fat Daddy said, shaking their hands.

"We cool man—where da niggah at?"

"His ass in the bedroom. Ah'm tryin ta figure out what ta do wit dis bitch right now."

"Handle ya business, man."

Leroy and Rodney headed for the bedroom and thirty seconds later emerged with Junebug draped across Rod's shoulder. Panic overcame Peaches when she saw them because she knew they were taking him to Big Ed.

"Man, what yaw doin?" she screamed.

"Bitch, you'd be better off closing your eyes and remembering nuthin," Leroy deadpanned.

"Please man, let mah man go," she begged. "I'll suck yo dick, let yaw pull a train on me ... jus let mah man go."

"Fat Daddy, handle da bitch an make sho she don't talk," Leroy said as he and Rod bounced.

That last statement caused Peaches to forget about Junebug and try to save her own life. She lifted her mug up to look at Fat Daddy and was met by a thundering right to the forehead. Through her glazed eyes she saw Fat Daddy lick his greasy lips while loosening his belt buckle.

"Close da doe, Troy—yaw get sloppy seconds," Fat Daddy grinned while mounting Peaches with his thumbnail dick.

9
MY PROPERTY

Angelo Tortellini waited patiently in line at the record section of the police department. The wait proved longer than he imagined because for each customer, staff would have to pull the police report, explain the situation, then listen to the person come up with every reason why their car should be released. He found many of the excuses to be hilarious because most people were outright lying in order to skip paying the fines, which amounted to almost a thousand dollars after the thirty-day hold on their vehicle was lifted.

Angelo, a trim and handsome twenty-five-year old, was living the American dream. Emigrating from Italy to the States with his brother Vito while teenagers, they began driving taxicabs. Working sixteen-hour days and saving every penny they could, they bought a limousine.

Vito served as chauffeur while Angelo lined up clients.

They operated their business from a rented studio apartment which they shared, and when Vito slept, Angelo drove, meaning their business operated twenty-four seven.

In three years' time, the Tortellini brothers had a fleet of twelve limos, eighteen employees, and were millionaires.

"Next in line," said the woman as Angelo stepped to the counter.

"Good morning," he greeted, "my name is Angelo Tortellini and I'm here to pick up my car."

"I'll need the license and registration," she prompted.

Angelo produced the documents.

"Sir, I have to pull the file," she said, "be right back."

Angelo took out his phone, punched a speed-dial button, and began conducting business on the spot. Speaking in a loud voice, he boomed instructions through the receiver.

"Sir, I have the report," the woman said, returning.

"I'll get back to you." He ended the call. "Yes ma'am, so what do I have to do?"

"Well, it says here that the limousine was impounded and is now being held as evidence."

"Wait a minute, exactly *what* are you saying?"

"You won't be able to get the car until the police are satisfied it was not involved in criminal activity."

"What sort of criminal activity?" Angelo's voice rose.

"It says here that the vehicle in question was possibly involved in a one-eighty-seven."

"Murder?!" he screamed.

"Sir, you'll have to calm down."

"I don't see how that's possible—there must be some

mistake. Can I talk to someone in charge?"

"I'll get my supervisor," she said as she walked away.

Angelo turned and, facing the long line of people, he let out a whistling sound. Wiping his brow, which had begun to perspire, he waited.

"May I help you, sir?" asked the boss, an older white guy who read the report as he spoke.

"I'm trying to find out what I have to do to get my car back," Angelo stated.

"Well, it says here that the vehicle in question was possibly used in a homicide and if that's the case, you won't be able to get it back until...."

"Until what?" he blurted out.

"Until it's been dusted for prints; forensics has a chance to comb the vehicle for blood, hair strands, or any other piece of evidence they may find; or your driver cooperates and tells what he knows. It says right here that he's uncooperative." The man showed Angelo the document.

"Oh, he'll cooperate alright, or be unemployed looking for another job!" Angelo shouted. "Where is he anyway?"

"They have him downstairs on the second floor, in homicide."

"Thank you," Angelo said then marched to the elevator.

"Next in line," stated the woman as her boss went back to his office.

Tortellini rode the elevator to the second floor cursing under his breath. The longer his limo stayed in limbo, the more money he would lose. It was hard enough finding and keeping qualified staff, much less those without a criminal history. This sort of mess was bad for business.

* * *

"Look Collins, we got you and you know it!" Johnson slammed his fist on the table for emphasis. "Just tell us who helped you kill Silky."

"Officer, how many times do we have to go over this? I don't know no Silky," Jason Collins whined.

"Would you like some cheese with that?" Hernandez asked.

"Cheese with what?" Jason returned.

"All that fucking whine you got?" His accent was heavy.

"I don't have any whine, man."

"You address him as Sir!" shouted Johnson.

Johnson and Hernandez had played the good cop/bad cop routine hundreds of times and could be considered masters of the game. This time Hernandez was the good cop while Johnson played the bad guy's role. It was working to perfection, and they knew it was only a matter of time before Collins sang like a bird.

Jason sat handcuffed to his chair looking petrified. A first taste of incarceration always produced that effect. His angular white face appeared pale. It had been a very long night.

"Look punk," Johnson continued, "all you got to do is tell us what you know—it can't be any simpler than that."

"But I'm telling you, I don't know nothing!" Jason screamed.

"OK, here is the deal, Jay—I can call you Jay, right?"

Hernandez' voice was soothing.

"Yes sir." Jason remembered Nate's warning.

A sudden knock on the door interrupted whatever words Hernandez was about to say. He opened it and greeted the boss, Edgar Lewis.

"May I speak with you guys?" Lewis asked.

Johnson and Hernandez both walked out and shook Lewis' hand. Closing the door behind them, Hernandez cut off his micro recorder. "What's up, boss?" he asked.

"Looks like we have some assistance."

"Assistance?" Hernandez looked puzzled.

"Yes Manny—Collins' boss, one Angelo Tortellini, is waiting in my office. The gentleman wants to claim his limo."

"I'm sure you told him that's impossible," Nate stated.

"Yes Nate, but he feels that if we allow him the opportunity to speak with our prisoner, he can coerce him to talk."

"That confident, huh?" Hernandez said.

"Convinced of it, Manny."

"OK, let's give it a shot," Johnson said calmly.

The threesome entered Lewis' office. Angelo was on his cell phone barking instructions. Upon viewing the officers coming, he ended the call.

"I'll get back to you," he said into the receiver.

"Mr. Tortellini," Lewis said, "meet detectives Johnson and Hernandez. They are the lead investigators on the case."

"How ya doin?" Angelo asked, shaking their hands.

"Fine sir," Johnson said before continuing, "I understand you'd like to have a few words with our prisoner?"

"Yes I would, if you will allow it."

"We have no problem with that if you'll agree to us being present and recording the conversation."

"Agreed." Angelo stated while rising from his seat.

Lewis smiled as he watched the three men enter the interrogation room. Somehow he felt confident that Tortellini would deliver—the guy had charisma. Besides, you don't become a multi-millionaire by being soft.

Jason's eyes grew large as saucers when he looked up and saw his boss follow the detectives into the room. Although he was older than Angelo, he gave him the utmost respect.

"Boss, you gotta get me outta here!"

"Calm down, Jason," Angelo said. "Before I can get these gentlemen to let you go, you have to cooperate. Just tell 'em what you know." Angelo sat next to Jason.

"I don't know nothing." Jason's voice was softer.

"Jason, now let me tell you what I know. I know for a fact that we ran a check on the woman who rented my limo and she doesn't exist, so you'll have to tell us everything that happened from the time you picked up your passengers, who they were, and any particulars you can think of. Do that, and you still have a job."

"OK boss, I'll do it for you." Jason caved in.

Angelo got up and stood next to Johnson and Hernandez, who had placed the micro cassette on the table and pushed the "record" button. Tortellini nodded to Jason, who began singing. Hernandez pulled his notepad from his sports coat.

"First, I met this guy named Leroy."

"What's his last name?" asked Hernandez.

"I don't know." Jason scratched his head.

"Where did you meet him?"

"At the courthouse."

"What happened?"

"He told me to drive his brother to Santa Rita, where he could pick up his personal belongings."

"That would be Ed Tatum?"

"He just called him Big Ed."

Manny jotted down "Ed Tatum" and "Leroy Tatum" on his notepad before firing off the next question.

"Then what did you do?"

"I drove him home, but he had an argument with his wife, and she pulled a knife on him."

"Did he hit her?"

"No, he had me drive him to Hayward. I took him to his mom's house."

"What did he do there?"

"I'm not sure—guess he took a nap or something."

"How long did you wait?"

"All day, maybe eight hours."

"OK," Hernandez said before a thought crossed his mind. "Did you leave at any time to grab a bite to eat?"

"No sir," Jason replied, "company policy states that you stay with the customer unless they say it's fine to leave. I munched on snacks." Angelo's chest swelled upon hearing Jason's response.

"What happened when Big Ed finally came out?"

"I took him to the coming-home party, a place called Club 99."

"He went in?"

"Yes."

"Continue," Manny prompted.

"I sat in the car and waited."

"What time did he come out?"

"Somewhere around midnight."

"What happened next?"

"They got in ..."

"Wait a minute," Hernandez interrupted, "who are 'they'?"

"Three of them. One was Big Ed; the other two were his brother Leroy and their friend Roderick, Rodney, something like that. Anyway, I took them one block over to the strip, where they stood outside watching the cars go by."

"Go on, you're doing fine."

"So Big Ed gets inside and leans over the seat. He tells me they need to use the car."

"Is that company policy?"

"No sir," Jason cautiously eyed an angry Angelo. "I'm sorry, boss, but those dudes were dangerous! Besides, he said he'd pay for any damages."

"What happened next, Jason?" Angelo demanded.

"Big Ed gave me a hundred-dollar bill and told me to wait at the diner. Next thing I know, these guys were hauling me off to jail."

"How much time passed before you came out from the restaurant?"

"About an hour."

"So you don't know when they brought the car back?"

"Not exactly."

"Excuse us for a minute."

Hernandez spoke more to Angelo than Jason as he and Nate left the room. They both knew they would have to release Jason, and that if Tortellini hadn't appeared on the scene, who knows how long it would have been before Jason cracked. Now they had fresh leads.

10
TWISTED FATE

Crystal dreamily woke around noon. She couldn't remember ever having slept so peacefully. Her body felt as if Big Ed were still inside, stretching her vagina past its limit. The girl now knew her theories on size were definitely wrong because after having experienced Big Ed, no small dick would ever satisfy her again.

Glancing at the clock, she rolled over, only to have her arm hit the pillow. Instantly her heart raced a mile a minute, hoping he hadn't left without saying goodbye. Dragging her beautiful naked frame out of bed, she attempted to take a step and nearly collapsed as her legs betrayed her body.

Holding onto the posts of her canopy bed, Crystal walked painfully to the restroom, delighted at the sight. Big Ed stood stark naked in her bathroom mirror, applying baby oil to his muscular body. As fine as he was, she only seemed to notice the weapon dangling between his legs.

"I thought you were gone," she said.

"Good morning to you too," he said as he kissed her cheek.

"Ooh baby, I'm sorry—good morning!" She hugged him.

"Now why would I leave without saying goodbye?"

"I don't know, guess I'm tripping."

"Guess so," he said, "how you feel?"

"I feel wonderful." Her voice rose three octaves.

"Did I satisfy you?" he asked, knowing the answer.

"Yes," she whispered, feeling his penis stiffen on her stomach.

Big Ed held her close while backtracking to the bed. Laying her down gently, he mounted. Crystal moaned upon feeling him penetrate then began kissing his massive chest as he plowed into her. She'd never had anyone come close to making her feel that way.

"Ooh baby, you feel sooo ... good inside of me, I love you."

Big Ed secretly smiled to himself because he knew she was sprung. Now he could have his way with her due to the fact in his mind it was just good sex, but to her it was love. Women always made the mistake of not distinguishing love from good sex. Blasting off a powerful load of cream into her well-lubricated hole, he rolled over on his back.

Crystal lay beside him gasping for breath while her body spasmed uncontrollably. Three minutes later, she was snoring up a storm. Big Ed smiled at his sleeping beauty then headed for the shower. Returning to the room fully dressed, he lightly shook her.

"Honey, wake up."

"Yes, baby," she answered huskily.

"I have a few runs to make—what's on your schedule?"

"Since I missed church, I don't have anything else to do."

"I was just making sure so I know you'll be here when I come back."

"I'll be here," she said. "Would you like me to fix you dinner?"

"That's cool."

"OK baby, wait a minute."

Crystal's hand fumbled around in the nightstand drawer before finally locating what she was seeking. "Here," she said, "these are my spare keys."

"Good—that way if you're not home I can let myself in."

"Yes, dear," she giggled.

"Hang this up for me."

Big Ed handed her his suit, kissed her on the cheek, and walked out the door. Crystal smiled when she heard his key turn the top lock. Picking up the phone, she dialed her sister's house.

"Peanut, girl, I'm in love!" she screamed into the phone.

She spent the next two hours thanking her sister for missing the wedding because that turn of events brought Big Ed into her life. Her sister didn't sound too excited on the other end of the line, but Crystal assumed it was because of her own set of problems.

Big Ed drove down the street congratulating his alter ego on the fine number he'd pulled on Crystal.

"Good shit, dog, you toe dat ass up!!"

Upon hearing his stomach growl, he realized that his body was telling him it's time to eat. Rolling to Giant Burgers on MacArthur near the Oaktown/San Leandro border, he ordered two cheeseburgers, fries, a slice of apple pie, and a soft drink, then went inside to sit on a stool.

His pager had been blowing up all morning, but he ignored it because he was busy taking Crystal's heart. It buzzed again now, forcing him to check the messages. Good news: Leroy and Rodney had successfully captured Junebug and were awaiting further instructions.

Opening his flip phone, Big Ed dialed his brother.

"Hello," Leroy answered.

"Hey bro, yaw got da niggah, huh?"

"Man, where you at? You know you still owe me foe Silky's ass," Leroy slurred. He was drunk.

"I got hung up yesterday, dude, but don't worry, you and Rod will be paid."

"Why dat niggah get sumpin? All he did was drove."

Big Ed heard Rodney arguing with Leroy in the background, then the next thing he knew, Rod was on the line.

"Man, tell dis dude ah get paid too!!" Rod screamed into the phone.

"Rodney, calm down, didn't I say you was covered?"

"Right, but dis fool. . . ."

"Be cool, man." Big Ed cut him off in mid-sentence. "Bofe yaw niggahs got scrill comin—now where yaw got Junebug at?"

"Right here wit us," Rodney answered.

"Looka here, I'll be dare in a minute after I get my grub on, dig?" Big Ed's voice rose.

"Ah hear ya talkin, boss."

"Now put dat clown of a brother back on da phone."

"Yeah, man?" Leroy said.

"Man, quit trippin off Rod."

"Awight bro."

"Ah should be dare in 'bout an hour."

"OK Eddie, everythang's copasetic."

"Later."

Big Ed hung up and began eating his meal. Thirty minutes later he cruised Sunnyside, waving at the usual assortment of street peddlers, dopefiends, and skeezers.

Barging in the door, he was surprised to find Junebug laughing and drinking beer with his captors.

"So you wanna whup mah ass, huh?" Big Ed dropped his overnight bag and made a move towards Junebug.

"Hole up, man." Junebug extended both arms with his palms turned upward. "Ah was just drunk."

"Well, now that liquor gone be da reason ah'ma whup yo ass."

"Wait a minute, man." Leroy stepped between Big Ed and Junebug. "We been talkin and Junebug done agreed to tell us all he know about Silky's operation."

"Fuck dat shit, Leroy, I'ont need da niggah!" Big Ed yelled.

"Yes you do, man—now listen foe a minute."

"OK, dis better be good."

Big Ed took a seat at the kitchen table, never taking his eyes off Junebug, who remained passive.

"Awight Junebug, go 'head." Leroy gave him permission to speak.

"It's like this, man"—Junebug took a swig of beer— "Silky ran his operation different than anything we know. He had hoes and gay boys distributing product from their homes, and he only used street-corner dealers to fool Big Ed."

"Is that right?" Big Ed stroked his chin.

"Right, man. See, the thang is, ah know all dose hoes so they'll be comfortable with me brangin dem da shit, but ah doubt if they'll work for you." Junebug finally looked Big Ed in the eye.

"Why you say dat?" Big Ed was curious.

"Cause dey don't know you. They know of you but they trusted Silky's slick ass—most of da hoes he was fuckin anyway."

"So you sayin you can keep 'em sellin?"

"I'll stake mah reputation on it." Junebug hit the sauce again.

"Would you be willin ta stake yo life on dat?" Big Ed's question was more of a threat.

"I'd have ta answer yes, seein ah ain't got no choice."

Big Ed pondered Junebug's statements, which confirmed his earlier theories that Silky had to be doing something different. Whether he could trust Junebug or not remained to be seen; the dude had vowed revenge.

"I'll tell you what, Junebug."

"Lay it on me, boss."

"I'mo give you a chance to prove yo mettle, but if you cross me, kiss yo life goodbye."

The look Big Ed directed at Junebug let everyone know he meant business. Rising up to retrieve his duffel bag off the floor, Big Ed opened it, handing Leroy and Rodney ten thousand each. Placing a generous amount of cocaine on a mirror, he took a straw and sniffed two humongous lines before passing it. The four men spent the next two hours snorting coke and devising strategy.

11
BLIND LOVE

"So where's this new man you've been telling me about?"

"Girl, you'll meet him," Crystal said to her sister, "and when you do, don't be giving the eye neither."

Crystal and her older sibling Peanut casually strolled through Bayfair Mall's food court. Peeping out the menu for Oriental cuisine, Peanut ordered chow mein, broccoli beef, and dry-fried ribs. Crystal went to the stand next to it and bought a slice of pizza.

The two sisters received more than their share of compliments while shopping and didn't seem to notice all the handsome men suddenly behind them in line. Like most men do, the dudes just admired the two fine women without uttering a word.

They assumed that these honeys had to have a man or men in their lives, so they just enjoyed the visual pleasure their eyes rested on. However, like always, there was a fool in the bunch. Dressed in a wrinkled black sweatsuit with a dirty shirt, faded black golf cap, and run-over tennis shoes, he assumed the role of mack daddy.

"Young lady, haven't we met befoe?" he said.

"I don't think so," Crystal responded.

"Naw naw, ah know ah done seen you somewhere." He stroked his chin. "Where you work at?"

"I don't think that's any of your business."

"Oh, it's like dat, huh? Ah'm just sayin ah thank ah know you."

"Like I said, I don't think so." Crystal felt like splashing the pizza in his face. "Let's find a table," she said to Peanut.

"Aw well, fuck you den, bitch—ain't like ahm tryin ta git at ya ugly ass, ah just thought ah knew you."

"Excuse me," Crystal stopped in her tracks, "I'm not your bitch and you don't know me!!"

"Man, leeb da gurl alone," spoke a snaggle-tooth dude who had to be his partner.

"Man, I ain't bothered nobody, ah jus thought ah knew her. Den she gone try ta shine me on like ah'm some punk-ass niggah. Shidd, ah got money...."

"Yaw ladies excuse mah friend," said ragged mouth. "He don't know no bettah."

"Thank you," Crystal responded.

The two derelicts walked away with the loud mouth staring back evilly at Crystal. She and Peanut chose a corner booth in the court and resumed their chat about Big Ed.

"What's his name?" said Peanut.

"Girl, I don't know that fool!" Crystal said, looking at the loud mouth.

"Not that clown," Peanut laughed, "your new man."

"Oh, his name is Edward."

"Kick the ballistics."

"Let me see . . . he's about six-feet-four, built like a warrior, cute—" she smiled, "and the best lover I've ever known."

"Oh really?" Peanut arched her brow.

"Really! Gurll, that man can do thangs in bed other men only dream about, OK?" she squealed.

The sisters chatted away freely for the next thirty minutes, with Crystal doing most of the talking. By the time they left, Peanut was dying to meet her sister's new beau. Stopping at the nail shop, they each got the manicure /pedicure combo.

They left the nail shop and rolled to the crib. Crystal inserted her key into the lock and they both entered her condo unit. Rap music blasted away from her stereo, meaning one thing.

"Girl, don't tell me he already has a key," Peanut said.

"Of course," Crystal responded while setting her packages on the floor. "Hi honey," she yelled, "I'm home!"

"Hey baby," Big Ed said, entering the room. Then he tongue-kissed her.

"Oh, excuse me!" she gasped. "This is my sister Peanut. Peanut, meet my man Edward; everybody calls him Big Ed."

"Nice to meet you, you look familiar—have we ever met?" he asked.

"I don't know, could be," Peanut returned.

"Hey, I have a friend here.... Homeboy!" he called out.

Junebug appeared in the hallway to greet the two sisters, holding a handful of CDs. The smile on his face disappeared instantly. Peanut felt as though she were about to puke.

"I have to use the restroom," she said.

"Baby, this is my boy Junebug," Big Ed announced.

"Hello Junebug—don't worry about my sister. I think it's the Chinese food she ate."

"No problem. It's nice to meet you, Crystal," Junebug said politely.

"Let me go check on her—you guys make yourselves at home."

Crystal knocked on the bathroom door. "Sister, you alright in there?"

"I'm fine," Peanut answered, then opened it.

"Gurll, that dude is fine," Crystal whispered, referring to Junebug.

"Looks ain't everything."

"Peanut, what's wrong with you?"

"Ain't nothing wrong, I guess my stomach doesn't agree with the food I ate."

"Well, you know what they say."

"What they say, sis?" Peanut's tone was sarcastic.

"Birds of a feather flock together."

"Meaning...?"

"If he's anythang like mah man—" she snapped her fingers for emphasis—"your heartbreak will be over. Let's go."

Crystal led the way to the living room then introduced Peanut properly to Junebug. Big Ed bear-hugged Crystal and asked, "What you got ta drank?"

"Just some wine—what would you like, baby?"

"I'd like you to go to the store with me so I can get some cognac for me and my homeboy."

"OK," she agreed. "Peanut, Junebug, you two get acquainted. We're going to the store. Did you want anything?"

"No," they said in unison.

Crystal grabbed her purse and headed out the door with Big Ed. The minute it slammed, Peanut tossed her purse on the sofa and stared daggers into Junebug's pleading eyes. Before she could speak, he did.

"Let me explain."

"Alright ... talk!" she screamed.

Junebug paced the floor trying to think of what to say. He knew this would not be easy.

THE HEAT IS ON

Johnson sat at his desk typing a report. It read as follows:

> *(5May) ATTN ALL UNITS: Arr for poss 187 of*
> *Duane "Silky" Johnson. Susp #1 Tatum, Edward*
> *AKA "Big Ed," 6'5, 300, lead/E. side emp. Susp #2*
> *Tatum, Leroy, 5'9, 200 LKA 96/Sunnyside. Susp #3*
> *Roderick/Rodney NLN, 5'11, 200 NFD. Susp's veh*
> *rented limo, should be considered armed & danger-*
> *ous. Contact me day/night when app.*
> *SGT. Johnson x4424*

TRANSLATION: Arrest Big Ed, Leroy, and "Rod" whose last name we don't know for the murder of Silky. Your best chance will be to get Leroy first because he hangs out around 96th & Sunnyside. They may try to engage in gun play, so be careful. Call me 24/7 when you get 'em.

E-mailing the report off to communications, Johnson

knew it would be only a matter of time before those three were in custody. The memo would be added to the Bulletin, a one-page document published daily by the Oaktown PD. It consisted of reports from throughout the department requesting or giving information.

All officers reporting for duty would read the Bulletin, so every cop on the force knew who to look for, what they'd done, their hangout locations, and criminal history. In effect, the Bulletin verified the fact that Five-O worked even while criminals slept.

Satisfied with his log-in, Johnson stretched his giant frame then took a swig of cold coffee from his personalized mug. Hernandez entered the room with that usual stoic expression on his face. The dude's stare could melt ice.

"What's happening, Nate?"

"Not much, Manny, just sending in my contribution to the Bulletin."

"Good deal man, now we'll get those assholes. What's our next move?"

"Let's talk to the vice squad—maybe they can give us a positive ID on this Rod guy."

"I'm with you, man."

The two detectives marched towards the vice squad office but before they could get there, they ran into a smiling face.

"Hello Derrick," greeted Johnson.

"How ya doin, sir?" the officer returned. He shook Manny's hand. "What's up?"

"Not much, just on our way to your old stomping grounds," Johnson answered.

"Looking for someone?"

"Yeah, suspect's name is Rod or some variation of that —hangs out with Big Ed and his brother Leroy."

"Rodney Gates," stated Derrick.

"You know the guy?" asked Hernandez.

"Put it like this, we've had a few run-ins. He hangs out in front of the grocery store on 85th & Bancroft."

"Come with us," Johnson ordered while pirouetting on his heels.

Derrick Boston followed the two senior detectives back to their office. Boston had gained the reputation of being the best vice officer OPD ever had, but since being reassigned to homicide, he'd only been given open-and-shut cases, and he yearned for some action.

Most detectives arrived for work dressed in outdated suits, but Boston dressed casually then changed into a suit once he got there. Today he wore blue jeans, a muscle shirt, golf cap, and sneakers. Most of his neighbors in the lily-white suburbs of Hercules considered him to be an athlete.

The trio entered Deputy Chief Lewis' office and stood at attention while he finished up a phone conversation. He ended the call then greeted the detectives.

"Afternoon fellas, I hope this is good news."

"We think so, chief," Johnson said. "Derrick has identified our third suspect as one Rodney Gates, hangs out in front of a store on 85th & Bancroft. With your permission we'd like Derrick to tag along with us while we look for the guy."

"What about the other two?" Lewis asked.

"We've put out an APB, sir."

"Good deal, Nate—let me know when you get 'em."

"Of course, Edgar. We wouldn't have it any other way."

They shook hands, with all four men laughing at the camaraderie between Nate and Edgar. Johnson had known Lewis since he first joined the force and served as his field training officer, meaning he'd shown him the ropes. He was proud to see Lewis rise rapidly in ranks and knew it would be only a matter of time before he was top dog, if not in Oaktown, then elsewhere.

"I'll need a few minutes to change," Boston said as they walked out.

"You're fine the way you are, Derrick," Johnson responded. "Besides, the old man can't chase 'em down like he used to."

Derrick grinned upon hearing Nate's remark because finally after weeks of desk work, he just might get some real action. They headed for transportation and checked out their standard navy-blue Crown Victoria. Boston hopped in the back.

Johnson got on 880 and rolled, exiting at 98th. Cruising the city streets, he hooked a left at Bancroft and parked on the corner of 87th. Hernandez handed Boston a set of binoculars, which he used to zoom in on the corner two blocks away. Boston adjusted the focus lever and scanned the crowd of thugs in front of the store.

"Bingo!" he shouted instantly.

"He's there?" Hernandez asked.

"Like a rooster in a hen house," Boston answered.

"OK, Derrick," Johnson spoke with authority, "you get

out and approach from this angle, we'll drive past, make a U-turn, then call him to the car. If he runs, he'll be coming your way."

"He would be wise to see what you want, Nate." Derrick cracked his knuckles.

The scene in front of the store was like most in the hood: D-boys along with wannabes drinking forties, smoking blunts, and harassing all female customers seeking to enter the store, which scared most people away. Someone always brought a boom box, so rap music blared loudly, while folks riding by were generally disgusted with what they saw.

Most people wondered how in the world store owners allowed this sort of chaos to occur. What they didn't know was that the store owners who complained, called the police, or confronted the hoodlums usually returned the next morning to find their place of business burned to ashes, courtesy of a pipe bomb.

Rodney stood in the middle of the pack acting like a kingpin. Since he'd provided all the liquor and dope, everyone was kissing his ass along with laughing at the jokes he told, even though most weren't funny. He'd been spending the money he got that morning from Big Ed like it was hot, and everyone knew he must have done something deadly to earn it. They didn't care but were curious.

"Five-O!" someone shouted.

People began drifting to their cars or down the street. The music stopped. Johnson eased the service vehicle ten feet in front of Rodney while Hernandez leaned out the open window.

"Rodney Gates?" Hernandez asked.

"Who wants to know?" Rod fronted.

"Step over here for a minute."

"For what?"

"We need to ask you a few questions."

Rodney bolted like a track star upon hearing the starter pistol in a race, while Johnson and Hernandez eased out of the ride adjusting their neckties. Once he looked up, Rodney saw Boston strolling casually in his direction. Stopping momentarily, he looked a smiling Boston in the eye.

"Give it up, Rod." Derrick cracked his knuckles.

"Fuck you!" Rodney shouted.

Contemplating a dash across the street, Rodney thought better of it due to heavy traffic. Derrick continued his stroll in Rod's direction. In a split second, Rodney turned around to see how close Johnson and Hernandez were, looked again at Boston, then sprinted up the driveway between two homes.

Boston flung his shades down and gave chase. There was a six-foot-tall wooden fence separating Rodney from what he considered freedom, which he scaled in one leap. Just as he was about to climb over, a pit bull leapt up, snapping at him, narrowly missing his neck.

Easing down, he turned to face a grinning Boston, who knew what transpired by the dog's barking. Procedure would be for the officer to train a gun on Rodney until Johnson and Hernandez arrived, but he was having none of that. That would be too easy.

"Give it up, Rod," Derrick said again while advancing.

Rodney threw his hands up in exasperation then bum-rushed Boston, each man grabbing the other's shoulders to seek an advantage. Boston jerked down on Rod's torso while simultaneously lifting up his knee, which connected with such force that it knocked the wind out of Rod.

His arms fell harmlessly to his side before his back exploded in excruciating pain due to the wicked elbow administered by Boston. Rodney sprawled to the ground on all fours, gasping for breath.

Boston snatched a handful of hair, which caused Rodney's head to snap up, and aimed a fist directly at his face. Rodney was helpless but happy to see Johnson and Hernandez amble up the driveway.

"Rodney Gates, you're under arrest!" Johnson shouted.

"For what?" Rodney asked defiantly.

"Suspicion of murder. Cuff 'im, Derrick."

Boston slammed Rodney's face into the grass, placed a knee on his back, then fitted his wrists with handcuffs.

"Suspicion of murder? Man, I ain't kilt nobody!"

"Read him his rights, Manny," Johnson instructed.

"You have the right to remain silent...."

Hernandez continued to read Rodney his Miranda Rights as they walked him back to the street. Onlookers slowly reappeared from their hiding spots while Derrick retrieved his shades. Rod's stomach bubbled over, causing him to vomit on the spot.

Rodney looked a mess. Grass clippings covered his face and hair, his shirt was ripped to shreds, knees on his pants soiled with mud, body hunched over in pain, and the crimson-colored vomit spewing from his mouth made everyone shake their head in pity. It was obvious to all that he'd eaten Chinese food because the beer mixed with sweet and sour sauce also contained scraps of rib meat along with onions, pineapple, bell peppers, and rice. The smell was horrible.

"Ah won't mah lawyer!" Gates screamed through his bloody gold teeth.

Boston eased Rod's head into the car as he shouted instructions to his boys. The word would reach Big Ed and Leroy before Five-O got to the freeway. Rodney settled back into his seat, riding in silence.

THE GAME PLAN

"I had no choice—it was either play along and show him Silky's operation, or die," Junebug explained.

"So after all those threats about killing Big Ed, you turned into a coward, huh?"

"Melody, that ain't it!" he shot back.

"The name is Peanut," she growled, "and don't you forget it."

"Oh, so Big Ed don't know you're Silky's girl?"

"That negro knows nothing about me except I'm his new woman's sister, and don't you get drunk and tell it."

They stood facing each other, Peanut staring hatefully into Junebug's eyes while he looked downward at the blue carpet. He never knew her nickname was Peanut because no one ever called her that, and the shock of her being Crystal's sister threw him for a serious loop.

"I ain't gone get drunk an say shit—you need to worry

about your sister," he whispered.

"My sister has been calling me 'Peanut' all her life, just like you called Duane 'Silky.' She ain't the one I'm worried about."

"And I am?" His voice rose.

"Junebug, look, we don't have time to argue."

"You da one arguing!"

"OK, OK!" She threw her hands in the air. "What we gotta do is develop a plan. You're with me, right?"

"You know I am," he stated.

"For now we'll just make him think we like each other."

"Cool."

"Now give me a hug."

Junebug turned up the volume on the stereo then stepped into Peanut's outstretched arms. They held each other tight as each one thought about Silky and revenge. Hearing the key inserted into the door lock, Peanut whispered, "Let's keep dancing."

Big Ed and Crystal walked in and both smiled immediately at the sight. Junebug's hand was on Peanut's behind as they slow-danced to the beat, appearing to be deep into each other's company.

"See, that's what I'm talking about," Big Ed chimed.

"They really seem to have hit it off," Crystal said.

She was amazed at the transformation in Peanut. Only minutes earlier, the girl acted as if she wanted no part of Junebug. Now she was letting him feel her up and down. Something just didn't seem right.

"Hey y'all." Crystal interrupted their dance.

"Oh, I didn't realize you guys were back," Peanut said

while straightening out her skirt.

"Don't pay us no 'tention," Big Ed cheesed. "We 'bout ta get our groove on too." Crystal elbowed his ribs, causing him to double over in laughter.

Big Ed grinned all the way to the kitchen, where he began pouring drinks for everyone. Junebug headed for the restroom while Crystal stared at her sister.

"What?" Peanut asked.

"You tell me, sis."

"Girl, I don't know what you're talking about."

"Peanut, something isn't right," she whispered.

"Crystal, everythang's fine—we started talking and realized we have a lot in common."

"Hey, why y'all whispering?" asked Big Ed from the kitchen.

"Just girl talk, honey," Crystal answered. "We'll talk later," she told Peanut under her breath.

Crystal joined Big Ed in the kitchen to assist with his drink-making. Junebug returned to the living room, joining Peanut on the sofa.

"They really seem to like each other," Big Ed told his woman.

"Yes, they do." She wasn't too convincing.

Crystal took two drinks into the living room, handing one to Junebug and the other to Peanut. When she went back, Big Ed pulled her into his arms. Crystal gazed into his eyes then met his lips in a very sensuous kiss.

"Let's make love," he whispered in her ear.

"What about them?" she whispered back.

"What about 'em?"

She felt his manhood pressing against her stomach and lost all sense of reason. Never being the type of woman to have sex with a man while people were in the next room, today she didn't care. Her body craved Big Ed, and at that moment, it controlled her mind.

They headed for the bedroom without saying a word. Peanut and Junebug heard the door close and shortly after that, noises they both knew well.

"Damn," Peanut said, "he got her ass sprung. I ain't never seen Crystal act this way."

"It happens to the best of 'em, baby."

"I know what I'll do," she said. "I'll feed Crystal all kinds of bullshit about how sprung I am on yo ass 'cause I know she'll run back and tell him." She said "him" with disgust.

"Why does it gotta be bullshit?" he asked.

"Dude, you know what I mean!" She laughed and hugged him.

The two continued to small-talk for a few more minutes then heard the bedroom door open as footsteps headed in their direction. Peanut embraced Junebug as Big Ed came into the room wearing only his pants. Looking wild-eyed, he put on his shirt as he spoke.

"I gotta raise, homes. Emergency."

"What's up?" asked Junebug.

"It's personal—I'll drop you off at the crib."

"That'll work."

"If you'd like I can take him home," Peanut volunteered.

"That's even better," Big Ed said while putting on his

socks and shoes. "I'll call you on your cell phone tomorrow," he told Junebug.

"OK," Junebug responded.

Big Ed rushed out the door without even going back into the bedroom.

"I'll be right back," Peanut told Junebug, then went into Crystal's bedroom. "Girl, you look a mess," she said to her sister.

Crystal's eyes had a glazed "I'm in love" look to them and her legs were spread wide into a vee shape under the covers. The room reeked of sex with its familiar funky scent. Peanut turned up her nose as she stared angrily at her sister.

"What's wrong?" asked Crystal.

"Girl, look at you, you need to get a grip."

"Peanut, why are you so angry?"

"Hey, I ain't angry. I just don't want my baby sister making an ass of herself behind no man."

"I'm not making no ass of myself."

"Crystal," she shouted, "having sex while we're in the next room qualifies as asshole, A-1!"

"Gurll, you trippin."

Peanut gathered up her things and stormed out of the room, slamming the door.

"Let's go," she told Junebug.

"OK," he said then downed his brandy.

"I'll get that fucker if it's the last thing I do."

Junebug lightly closed the door then trailed an angry Peanut to her car. He understood totally why she was so upset. Not only was Big Ed responsible for her man's death, he also had her sister cuckoo for coco puffs. That was a double whammy.

"Junebug, I want you to tell me everything you know about that ass—where he goes, sleeps, hangs out, parties, don't leave out nothing!"

"I was gonna do that anyway."

"Well . . . start talking."

Peanut rolled away in her beat-up lemon listening intently to Junebug, who told everything he knew about Big Ed. The more he talked, the more a plan began to formulate in her brain. Revenge would be sweet, or so she thought.

Meanwhile, Big Ed sped down Jauna to Bancroft. Running many yellow lights, he made a right on 82nd and another at MacArthur. Hooking a left at the first stoplight, he cruised into Alvingroom Court.

Alvingroom, a 150-unit gated community that resembled military housing, was located in the deep eastern part of town. One block from Castlemont High, it sat on a dead-end street. There was a security booth at the entrance but security was never there, so you could come and go as you pleased. Big Ed rolled past the security booth then parked at the end of the court. This spot served as the "cookhouse" where all cocaine was converted from powder into freebase rocks.

Getting out of his Benz, he marched up the steps and used his key to gain entrance into the two-bedroom unit. Leroy, Damon, and Muggsy, along with the three cookers, greeted him.

"Five-O got Rod, man," Leroy said.

"Where?" Big Ed asked.

"Picked him up on da conah—ah knowed dat niggah should'a laid low!" Leroy was angry.

"Calm down, Leroy, ahmo get 'im out."

Before the conversation went any further, Big Ed's cell phone rang. Once he hung up, he dialed another number then spoke in hushed tones, grinning broadly. Everyone grinned back because they knew he must have received good news.

14
LINEUP

Jason Collins sat inside the lineup room staring intently at his feet as they wiggled involuntarily under the pressure he was feeling inside. Angelo Tortellini placed a hand on his shoulder while taking a seat to his right.

Hernandez was at the control panel programming the television monitor, microphone, lighting, and videotapes. The tapes would be used as evidence upon positive identification. Johnson pulled up a chair next to Jason and began softly explaining the process.

The lineup was a procedure where the witness attempted to identify the suspect amongst a group of six. There were two types. The first was visual, which consisted of mug-shot photos of criminals with similar facial features, all taped on a folder for display. Five-O nicknamed this form a "six-pack" due to the way only faces were displayed.

The second type was a physical lineup where six inmates of similar height, weight, and facial features, including the suspect, were lined up side by side behind a one-way mirror. After the inmates carried out a series of maneuvers such as turning sideways, saying a specific phrase, and stepping up then back, the witness would attempt to pick out the correct suspect. Johnson and Hernandez always preferred this type of lineup because the results carried more weight in court.

Inmates loved participating because if they were incorrectly chosen, their cellmate just might beat his case. They also were treated to an extra brown bag lunch along with a guarantee that if they were pointed out by the witness, it would have no effect on their own charges.

"Alright Jason," Johnson whispered, "just be calm and take your time."

"I'll do my best, sir," Jason said while wiping his perspiring forehead.

Hernandez turned off the lights and locked the door, leaving the foursome in a darkened room. Next, he activated the spotlights in the lineup room then picked up the telephone and called downstairs to let the jail staff know they were ready.

The jailers marched the prisoners into the room single-file then stood off to the side. Rodney Gates was assigned the number-four position. Once all the prisoners were in place, Hernandez began.

"Gentlemen, turn to your left, please." They all did it. "OK, now turn to your right."

"Look closely, Jason, and try to remember anything

that stood out," Johnson cooed.

"Now, I want each of you to step up three paces then say, 'let me use the ride, man'—number one, you're first."

As each man went through the routine, Jason cringed. Even though Big Ed requested use of the ride, Jason knew who Rodney was and could finger him in an instant, but his brain reminded him how dangerous those guys seemed on that fateful night. The fact that Angelo had promised him a supervisor's position training new employees only increased the pressure.

He could sure use the extra money for his family, but at what cost? In the darkened room, Jason was shaking like a leaf. However, greed got the better of him, as it does most people.

"It's number four," he said loudly.

"You're positive?" Johnson double-checked.

"Yes, number four."

Jason spoke so loudly that the prisoners heard his response due to Hernandez' failure to cut off the microphone. They all gave Rodney a "man, we tried" look then were marched back downstairs to their cell. Rodney glared through the window not seeing anything, but Jason felt as though he were looking directly at him. His body shivered.

"Good job, Jason," Angelo said as he patted his back. "Now tomorrow when you come in, we'll start your supervisor training."

"Thanks boss," Jason replied meekly.

"Call me Angelo from now on."

Jason knew Angelo's only interest was in having his

limousine returned, along with the free publicity his company would receive for assisting with the case. Johnson and Hernandez thanked them both then showed them the exit.

* * *

Rodney returned to the holding cell furious. Although he didn't see the witness, he knew it was Jason. Roughly snatching the phone receiver from its holder, he placed a collect call to Big Ed's cellular.

"Talk to me," Big Ed stated in his normal dry tone.

The usual taped message informing him that the call was collect greeted Big Ed, who patiently waited until being instructed to push button number five in order to accept the charge.

"Talk to me, Rod."

"Dude, they picked me up on a humbug."

"What dey charge you wit?"

"Nuttin yet, but dey did put me in a lineup."

"What happened?"

"You know dat clown who drove da limo?"

"Yeah yeah."

"That fool fanga'd me out, man."

"Is that right?" Big Ed stroked his chin.

"Yeah dog, he shouted da shit. Ahma get his ass."

"Check it Rod, when dey interrogate, you know nuthin!"

"Got dat, dog."

"Stay cool, bro. I'll bail you out soon as dey post it."

"Propah," Rodney said with confidence.

They ended the call then Big Ed searched his wallet

furiously. Finding the piece of scrap paper he sought, he dialed.

"Hello."

"I got a job for you." Big Ed was direct, whispering.

"Kick the ballistics."

"White boy, drive a limousine, name's Jason."

"What company?"

"I'ont know dog, but it is dat company run by dose Italian dudes."

"I know them well."

"Handle it wit da quickness, man, an I'll throw in an extra five grand."

"That serious, huh?"

"Ah need him offed yesterday."

"You got it."

Big Ed hung up the phone and smiled to himself. He knew Jason was history now, and with no eyewitness, Five-O had no case because defense attorneys could not question a dead man. Turning to his boys, he grinned broadly. They returned the smile, happy to know that what had been a tension-filled day was once again peaceful.

SEARCH & CHASE

Johnson and Hernandez arrived for duty at five in the morning on what normally would be their off day. Meeting them were members of the gang unit, vice squad, and warrant detail. The group totaled twenty, and most were dressed in SWAT gear. The scene resembled a tactical strategic planning session before a drug raid, but today they were only looking for two people.

"Ladies and gentlemen," Johnson began, "the pictures being passed out to you are those of Big Ed Tatum and his brother Leroy. Shoot only if you have to because we need these two alive."

"Sarge, what about anyone else we nab?" asked one of the officers.

"We'll arrest any and everyone, but our main concern is the Tatum boys," Johnson answered before continuing. "They should be considered armed and dangerous, so be careful; however, we would like them alive."

Hernandez took center stage. "You'll notice the mug shot papers also contain addresses of the locations we'll raid. Most of them are drug houses—that's why we invited vice to our party." Everyone laughed. "Since you all know the drill, it should be a piece of cake. Any questions?" The room was silent. "Good. Nate?"

"Let's roll!" Johnson boomed.

The room emptied as officers scurried to their assigned vehicles. Johnson, Hernandez, Derrick Boston, and his partner Maria Jimenez hopped in their car and waited as the SWAT van, squad cars, and vice boys lined up in the caravan. Rolling off, their first destination was Big Ed's home.

Parking down the block, everyone took their assigned positions. Officers covered the front, sides, and rear of the home. Communication was done by way of radio transmitter headsets with an arm piece extending to the mouth. Johnson gave the go-ahead.

Three officers scurried up the walkway carrying a battering ram. The first one knocked loudly and shouted, "POLICE! OPEN UP!"

Shirley awoke from a peaceful sleep to the sound of her front door being demolished. Having been through the drill before—one month ago, to be exact—she remained in bed. Since the children were spending the night at their grandparents' house, she was home alone.

Hearing her windows being smashed, loud yelling from all the officers raiding her home, and the general chaos they created, she smiled knowing that her husband was in trouble again. She hated his ass and would help them if they only asked.

The bedroom door was kicked in so violently that one of the hinges broke. Shirley looked up into the trained guns at her face still grinning.

"Get your hands up where we can see them!" shouted the officer.

"If it ain't my old friends Lamont and Hoolio!" she roared.

Lamont and Julio were characters from the "Sanford and Son" sitcom, with Lamont being the son and Julio the Latino neighbor. Johnson and Hernandez knew exactly what she was joking about.

"Mrs. Tatum, we have a warrant to search the premises and arrest your husband," Johnson spoke while motioning for the officers to lower their weapons.

"All you gotta do is ask me and I'll help you get his ass. Yaw don't need ta fuck up mah goddamn home. Just did dat shit lass month." She laughed again.

"You tink dis funny?" Hernandez shouted.

"Oh, Hoolio speaks English? I didn't know that!"

Hernandez made a move towards the bed but Johnson grabbed his arm.

"Cool it, Manny."

Johnson instructed the female officers on the scene to stay in the room and watch Shirley's every move while she got dressed. Ten minutes later, the search was complete, with Five-O and their dogs turning up nothing. As the police units pulled off to the next location, Shirley stood on the porch giving her neighbors her best Adele Gibbons routine:

"See, dey done fucked up mah home again lookin fa dat low-life'd muthafucka who calls hisself mah kids' daddy. Who gone pay foe dis shit? Ah'mo sue da mutha-fuckin city, dat's what ahma do!"

The police caravan rolled to Leroy's home next. The d-boys lurking in the shadows saw the procession heading their way and got ghost. By the time Five-O parked down the street and officers began to get in place, the block was deserted.

Using the same tactic as they did at Shirley's home, everyone assumed their position. The battering ram smashed the front door, windows were kicked in, back door rammed open, and the place swarmed with cops. All for naught: the apartment was empty.

Since there was no evidence on the scene, Johnson in-structed the officers to gear up and head to the next loca-tion, which was the cookhouse in Alvingroom.

The special force unit (their tag) rolled quietly into Alv-ingroom Court. Parking near the security gates, everyone got into their positions. The previous raids had all offi-cers in an attack frame of mind, so everyone was ready.

Leroy slept peacefully on the sofa. He knew from the arrest of Rodney that it was only a matter of time before Five-O would be after him. He mistakenly thought they were unaware of the cookhouse. Restless and tired, he got up and went to the bathroom.

Glancing out the window while pissing, he spotted the rollers parking their vehicles. Knowing they were after him, Leroy quietly slipped out the back door and ran to the creek. As the police scattered in all directions surrounding the unit, Leroy ran right by them down the creek without anyone being the wiser.

Since there was only one way into or out of Alvingroom, Derrick Boston elected to stay behind his fellow officers and serve as a last line of defense just in case anyone slipped through the cracks.

Leroy climbed up the creekbed, surveyed the scene, and upon seeing the coast clear, sprinted through the gate. Derrick, who was positioned in front of the SWAT van, heard what he assumed to be footsteps. Peering around the van, he saw a man flying past the gate.

"Hey!" he hollered. Leroy kept running. "Police! Stop or I'll shoot!"

Leroy had no intentions of stopping, but upon hearing the threat of being shot, he turned around. What he saw startled him because half a block away was an officer limbering up as if he were getting ready for a championship race. His gun was not drawn.

Boston announced over his transmitter that the suspect, Leroy Tatum, was fleeing the scene, then took off. A former sprint champion in high school and reigning eight-hundred-meter champ at the Police Olympics, Derrick loved to run.

Leroy crossed MacArthur, veered left, then ran behind the 200 building at Castlemont High. He noticed Boston crossing MacArthur and gaining ground rapidly. Knowing instantly he would not outrun this guy, he jumped a six-foot chain-link fence and headed down what was a familiar spot, the creek.

"Suspect headed westward down the creekbed, I need

backup at Ritchie and Bancroft—go east and we can trap him. I'm still in pursuit!" Derrick shouted through his transmitter before scaling the fence.

Upon hearing Boston's message, Johnson, Hernandez, and Maria Jimenez left with the quickness. There were six people inside the cookhouse caught totally off guard. The vice unit assumed control and arrested them all, along with a large cache of drugs.

The creekbed ran from 84th to Richie, five city blocks. Homes were lined on each side with chain-link fences separating them from the creek. Dark, dingy tunnels ran under the cross streets, which posed a danger due to poor visibility. Muddy water covered two feet of the basin floor, along with trash and leaves. To top it off, overhanging tree branches plus weeds sprouting up through the cracks gave the place a jungle-like atmosphere. Boston saw his quarry zigzagging through the maze and knew that Leroy would make it to the first tunnel before he caught up.

Lifting his flashlight from its socket on his utility belt, Boston sloshed through the water slowly. Once he arrived at the tunnel, he moved his flashlight in a sweeping motion, peering intently for any movement. Seeing none, he crouched down low and prepared to enter.

Hearing a crackle of leaves from above, he looked up, only to be greeted by Leroy's foot to his head. The force of the blow knocked Derrick down, left him dizzy, and caused his flashlight to fall harmlessly into the water. Scrambling to regain his footing proved fruitless because Leroy connected with a crushing blow to his jaw.

Hurt and dazed, Boston felt Leroy's hand trying to lift

his revolver from its holster. He threw a wicked forearm that caused Leroy to bite his tongue, then finished it off with a straight right to the mouth. Rising up tall, he cracked his knuckles.

"Oh, you wanna battle, huh?" he sneered at Leroy.

"Ahmo whup yo ass punk, show yo sumptin," Leroy answered with blood pouring from his lips.

The two men faced off, circling each other slowly with their fists balled up. Leroy threw a roundhouse right that hit nothing but air. Boston ducked, caught him on the chin with an uppercut, then finished it off with a picture-perfect left hook that sent Leroy flying face-first into the mud.

Placing his knee in the small of Leroy's back, Derrick slapped the handcuffs on his wrists, lifting him roughly to his feet.

"You're under arrest, fool!" he shouted.

"Take da cuffs off an finish da job, or is you scared?"

"Suspect in custody," Boston spoke through his transmitter, "meet me at Castlemont."

"Just lack ah thought, you a punk."

Derrick rubbed the side of his face, feeling Leroy's footprint, which caused his temper to boil over. He set his foot on Leroy's behind and kicked it hard, giving Leroy a running start back to the school.

"When ah get out, ahmo whup yo ass!" Leroy shouted through his bloody mouth.

All the way back to the school Leroy continued to make promises of a definite ass-whipping that Boston could look forward to. Boston ignored his threats while steadily shoving him to their destination. Once they arrived at the fence Johnson, Hernandez, Jimenez, and several other officers began clapping.

Derrick took what Leroy thought was a bow, then lifted him up in the air by the knees and hoisted him onto the top of the fence. Nate and Manny pulled him to their side of the fence carefully—they didn't want cuts on his body where he could claim police brutality.

"When ah get out, ahmo whup yo ass, punk!" Leroy hollered one last time.

All of the officers on the scene laughed at Leroy's weak threat of vengeance because they knew if he was gonna "whup" ass, he would have done so in the creek. Easing him into a squad car, they took Leroy Tatum to jail.

Johnson wheeled the Crown Victoria in front of headquarters and grinned broadly. Getting out quickly, he and Hernandez summoned two uniformed officers as their backup. Jaywalking (more like running) into the bail bond establishment, they came out grinning with their suspect handcuffed. Now all they had to do was fit the puzzle pieces together.

SQUARE ONE

Big Ed awoke after a peaceful sleep and smiled. Crystal's head was bobbing up and down hungrily on his penis, causing it to stiffen. With catlike quickness Big Ed spun her on her back and penetrated forcefully. Cupping his arms under her shoulders, he banged away with all his might. Crystal's eyes rolled up into her head and her breathing momentarily stopped. Her body was on fire, feeling as though it would explode any second.

The swiftness and brute force of his sexual attack made him ejaculate after only two minutes, but Crystal thought it more like two hours. Her legs felt like jelly and her brain was numb.

Rising slowly off the bed, Big Ed went to take a shower. Crystal gazed lovingly at her cream saturating his meat and felt her legs quiver. They were shaking uncontrollably.

"No man has ever made me feel this way," she said throatily.

"I love you too, honey," he said while walking out.

She was in seventh heaven, lying there while his cum slowly dripped down the crack of her behind. Big Ed took a shower, ironed his clothes, ate leftover pizza in the refrigerator, then returned to the room rubbing cologne on his neck and face. Crystal was naked on top of the covers, snoring loudly.

"Yo ass is mine," he stroked his ego while staring at her lovely frame. "Bitch is phine," he agreed with himself then shook her lightly.

"Yes, honey," she said.

"What are your plans for today?"

"I don't have any, I'm on vacation, why?"

"Because I need to use your car for a minute."

"Anything for you, love." She handed over her keys, still feeling him inside of her.

Kissing Crystal on the cheek, he bounced, locking the door behind himself. Taking the elevator to the underground parking garage, he located her car and got inside. It was a brand new '93 Camry, black on black, and in desperate need of washing.

Big Ed adjusted the seat, started the engine, and rolled, pushing the garage door opener as he drove slowly toward the gate. Turning right, he hooked a left at the BART station, cruised down San Leandro Boulevard, then veered right onto Marina.

Heading to Doolittle Drive, he stopped at the gas station and filled up the tank, receiving the free wash coupon.

Taking the rear position of a four-car line, he searched for a rap tape while inching forward.

"Bitch ain't got no music in dis muthafucka," he cursed.

Adjusting the radio to KMEL, which served as the Bay Area's number-one rap station, he reclined in the seat bobbing his head to the Hammer jam "Can't Touch This." After inserting extra quarters into the slot for wax and dry service, he pulled into the pit.

When he exited, the car was clean as new money. Now he could roll. Big Ed joined the flow of traffic on 880 heading to Hayward and his parents' house. Since his parents lived closer to 580, he had to exit at Winton and travel crosstown to reach his destination.

Cruising past Southland Mall, the County Courthouse, City Jail, and downtown, Big Ed made a right on D Street, then another on Second. Riding uphill, he passed the back of Hayward High, glancing at their nickname—"Farmers"—scribbled in giant letters on the gymnasium facade.

Two blocks later he eased the car to a stop, got out, and went to the side door entrance of the garage. His parents were gone, causing him to smile with relief because he wouldn't have to hear any of his father's lectures. Elroy Tatum never let up on the sermons. As far as he was concerned, Big Ed and Leroy were failures in life because they chose the easy way out, selling drugs.

Closing the door behind him while flicking on the lights, Big Ed went to a wall cabinet that held motor oils, brake fluid, antifreeze, and several other car-care items. It had a padlock on it but that didn't matter because Big Ed lifted the entire unit from the wall and placed it on the floor. It had been secured by hooks built on the back, which slid neatly into slots on the original wall.

Staring him in the face were three shelves of guns, gigantic zip-lock bags of cocaine, and stacks of cash wrapped with rubber bands. Each stack contained ten thousand dollars, with the total amounting to more than two hundred grand.

Big Ed grabbed two stacks of money off the shelf then returned the cabinet to its normal place. Leaving as swiftly as he arrived, he jumped in Crystal's ride and drove away. As he hit the corner, his parents drove right past him, not recognizing their son in Crystal's car.

"Good timing, dog," he said to himself.

Joining the crowded procession of cars on 580 whose occupants were heading to work, he cruised to Oaktown, exiting at 12th Street. Rolling through town, he parked on 13th Street right in front of the Tribune building, dropped a quarter into the meter, then headed across the street.

The location was a small mailbox service sandwiched between a barber shop on the right and a beauty parlor on the left. Big Ed placed one ten-gee bundle into an envelope, lifted a key from his trousers, then unlocked mailbox number 785, shoving the package inside it.

With his stomach growling, he walked down the block to Broadway and strode into Burger King. Ordering enough food for three people, he copped a squat and chowed down. As he ate, he contemplated his next move.

First, he would hook up with Junebug (whom he felt still had to prove he was down) then get a bail bondsman for Rodney in hopes of gaining his release. After that, he'd check his dope houses and find Leroy. Lifting his cellular from his jacket, he dialed Junebug's number.

"Hello?" Junebug was still asleep.

"Yo dog, it's me."

"Whatup playa?"

"I'm eatin right now but can pick you up in about fifteen minutes."

"OK, I'll be on the corner of 8th & East 24th."

"That'll work." Big Ed ended the call and finished his meal.

Seeing Silky's operation firsthand, he understood why the boy was successful. Most of his associates were women, all of which were phine. Big Ed envisioned himself riding many of them. Smiling, he polished off his breakfast and cut out with no clue that Leroy had now joined Rodney in the slammer.

Junebug jumped out of bed and did a quick sponge bath of his face, underarms, genitals, and butt. Splashing on cologne, he removed the stocking cap from his head, got dressed, and bounced. He didn't want to start the day off wrong by having Big Ed wait. He also didn't want him to know where he lived.

Decked out in money-green slacks, matching silk shirt, green and white Stacy Adams along with socks and blazer to boot, Junebug stood on the corner with his jacket draped across his shoulder, posing like a male model. Many of the women at the bus stop across the street ogled at the fine young brother waiting patiently for what they assumed was the bus heading in the opposite direction.

Big Ed rolled up on the block in Crystal's car. Junebug,

not recognizing the ride, peered into the window. The door locks thumped upon Big Ed hitting the release button, and Junebug got inside. Continuing up East 24th, the Camry hooked a right on 14th Avenue.

"Man, you bought another car?" Junebug asked.

"You look like you ready to go partying, dude." Big Ed gazed at Junebug's outfit, ignoring his question.

"Just my daily attire, dog—what's on the agenda?"

"We gonna make the rounds, but first I hafta see if I can bail out Rod."

"Five-O got Rod?"

"Yeah, they got his ass."

"For what?"

"Some bullshit charge—he'll be out foe noon."

Junebug let out a whistle while reclining in his seat. Big Ed sped down 14th to East 12th, veered right, and cruised past Laney College onto 8th Street. Junebug was silently taking in the scenery while listening to Public Enemy's latest rap single.

Turning left on Washington, Big Ed made another left at 7th, parking on the left-hand side of the street. 7th Street housed Five-O headquarters and North County jail on the right, Bailbond Row on the left.

Bond Row consisted of eight neon-lit offices. Operating twenty-four seven, they were a happy sight for family members hoping to get a loved one released from jail. To those with no credit or cash, it was a mirage because bond offices did not conduct business on sympathy or promises to pay later.

"Wait right here," Big Ed said before Junebug had time to unfasten his seatbelt.

Big Ed entered Precious Bonds, taking a chair in front of the desk. The lone person in the office was a heavyset black lady with a pleasant personality. She held up one finger, letting him know that her call was nearly complete as he placed a paper bag on the desk then flipped through the pages of an outdated *Jet* magazine.

Hearing footsteps approaching rapidly behind him, Big Ed turned around in his chair, only to stare directly into the nine-millimeter handguns that Johnson and Hernandez had trained on his cranium.

"Freeze or you're dead!" Hernandez shouted.

"Man, what yaw wont now?" Big Ed said while slowly raising his hands in the air.

"You're under arrest," Johnson answered, cautiously approaching.

"Arrest? For what?"

"Suspicion of murder. Read him his rights, Manny."

The two detectives led Big Ed out of the bail bond office with him proclaiming innocence. On the curb outside, Junebug's hands were cuffed, torso hugging the hood of the car, three uniformed officers creating a triangle around him. The lady in the bond office witnessed the entire scene, then headed for the phones—she would have some interesting gossip to spread that day.

Before she sat, she noticed the bag Big Ed had placed on her desk. It was a small brown paper bag that appeared to contain a sandwich. Peering inside, her eyes grew big as bo-dollars because it was full of money. Counting it, she let out a whistle. The gossip would have to wait—she called her boss.

17
A WHAMMY

As Big Ed was escorted across the street, he was surprised to see his brother being led into the station too. Looking over his shoulder, he yelled to a now-free Junebug to take the car to his woman's house and tell her what had gone down. Johnson thought Junebug looked familiar but just couldn't place him.

Junebug had to wait until the officers conducted a thorough search of the ride, along with checking to see if he had any outstanding warrants before they allowed him to leave. He didn't know which woman Big Ed referred to, so he pulled the registration from the glove box. Seeing Crystal's name as the registered owner, he started the engine then hit 880 towards San Leandro.

Easing to a stop on Juana Street, he parked and got out. Peanut rolled up behind him, joining him on the sidewalk.

"What are you doing in my sister's car?" she asked.

"Bringing it back," he answered.

"Where's Crystal?"

"I don't know—hope she's in the house, if not I'll give you her keys."

"Wait a minute, Junebug—I seem to be missing something. Let me start over. How did you get Crystal's car?"

"I got it from Big Ed, who just got arrested."

"He did?"

"Yes."

"For what?"

"I think they got him for Silky's murder. They got his brother Leroy too."

"Good!" she shouted. "That's what the bastard deserves!"

Glancing into Crystal's ride, Peanut spotted a set of keys in the cup holder.

"Where are Crystal's keys?"

"Right here," Junebug said as he dangled them in her face.

"Then whose keys are those?" she asked, pointing inside the car.

"I don't know, honey—probably Big Ed's."

"Give me the keys," she demanded.

Junebug handed over Crystal's keys to a smiling Peanut, who opened the car door and lifted the second set from their resting place. He had no idea why she wanted Big Ed's keys but knew her intentions were not nice.

"Why are you taking his keys?"

"You'll see," she said. "It must be my lucky day. I have a spare set to Crystal's house, so I'll just leave her keys on the coffee table."

"Honey," Junebug whined, "I told Big Ed I would give Crystal the four-one-one on what went down."

"Tell his ass you got a flat tire or something."

Peanut used her spare key to the entry gate, marched through the courtyard, then let herself into Crystal's condo. Junebug trailed behind wondering what she was up to. He silently knew he should not have let her get her hands on Big Ed's key ring.

To say they looked odd would be an understatement. Whereas he was fly to the max, she wore black jeans, turtleneck sweater, tennis shoes, and golf cap. Suddenly he felt overdressed.

Peanut unlocked Crystal's door, placed her keys on the kitchen countertop, then strutted to the bedroom. Seeing her sister lying on top of the covers butt naked with her legs gapped wide open almost caused her to puke. Disgusted, she turned to leave, only to bump into Junebug, who was devouring the sight like a blind man who had just regained vision.

"Niggah, if you don't stop lusting my sister, you'd better," she huffed.

"Damn," Junebug said while soaking in the view.

"Let's go." Peanut grabbed his arm and whisked him from the room.

Junebug glanced over his shoulder for one last peek at Crystal's fine frame before being jerked from the doorway. Peanut was in no mood for fun and games, which he realized from her demeanor and actions.

"Where we goin?" he asked outside.

"You'll see soon enough," she returned.

"What are you gonna do wit dose keys?"

"Junebug, stop the goddamn twenty questions and come on."

"Ah ain't got no twenty questions, just one."

"Well, ah ain't answerin it; you'll find out soon enough."

"It must be my unlucky day," he said dryly.

"How so?"

"First, Big Ed gets arrested, then I run into you, and last but not least, you take the man's keys."

"Don't worry, honey, revenge will be sweet," she laughed.

They got inside her bucket, which was a beat up '88 Accord supposedly teal in color but in desperate need of a paint job. Junebug reclined his seat, cringing at the filthiness of Peanut's ride. Coffee cups, trash, and clothes were everywhere, dust covered the dashboard, and there was so much smudge on the window you could write your name on it from the inside.

Peanut didn't seem to mind, starting the ignition, hooking a U-turn, and speeding up to 580. She entered the freeway heading east when Junebug opened his mouth to speak.

"You'll see when we get there," Peanut answered before he could ask the question.

Junebug rolled his eyes up in his head and resumed staring into traffic. Peanut got off at Foothill, hooked a left on D, then a right on Second Street.

"I know we ain't goin where ah thank we goin," Junebug stated uncertainly.

"Yep," Peanut giggled, "ta his mama's house."

"Girl, you done lost yo mind—what we goin up here foe?"

"I followed that fool up here this morning and saw him get something out of the garage. I figure it had to be money or dope, maybe both. If so, we gone find it, then break the bank!" She laughed heartily.

"We'll be dead before we get to enjoy it."

Parking down the block across from Hayward High's football field, she eased to a stop. Since Big Ed's parents' car was still in the driveway she elected to wait it out. Junebug was antsy due to the fact this was a mission he hoped to never attempt, much less accomplish.

"Why you so scared?" Peanut turned to face Junebug.

"'Cause you don't know what you doin."

"Yes I do," she quipped.

"Right," he deadpanned.

"Man, you need ta quit trippin."

"Bitch, ah ain't trippin, ah jus happen to love life."

"And I don't?" she asked loudly. "Matter of fact, who you callin a bitch?"

"Obviously not!" he yelled, "an ah'm callin yo ass a bitch, bitch!"

Peanut and Junebug continued their argument for the next twenty minutes. To teenagers cutting class or residents walking their dogs, it appeared to be a lovers' quarrel, so no one paid them much attention. The moment Junebug made up his mind to whip her ass, Big Ed's parents walked out of their house.

"There they go," whispered Peanut. Junebug felt a lump form in his throat as he watched the elderly couple drive

off. He knew that what Peanut had in mind meant instant
death to both of them and he wanted no part of it. Somehow he had to convince her that what she was about to do
was not wise. His life depended on it.

"You ain't comin?" she asked while getting out.

"Nope," he shot back unconcerned.

"Suit yourself, you pussy," she snarled angrily.

"Yo mama!" he hollered.

Peanut strutted to the garage door ignoring the obscen-
ities Junebug hurled at her. She was on a mission. He
watched her fumble around at the door, hoping that the
keys she possessed did not belong to Big Ed. Just when he
thought she had failed, she went inside.

Ten minutes elapsed and still there was no sign of Peanut,
so Junebug reluctantly got out and went to see what was
taking her so long. Smiling at the sight, he entered laughing because she sat slumped on a workbench looking de-
feated.

"What you laughing at, you coward?"

"I'm laughing at you, girl. Ah tole you dis was a mistake
from the get-go but naw, yo ass don't listen."

He was animated with his movements, slapping the
back of his right hand into the palm of his left, smiling
like a circus clown, and generally acting giddy. Peanut
glared at her dead honey's homeboy thinking nothing but
coward. How could Silky run with an ass like that? she
thought. Even though she came up empty, he was afraid
to see. Staring at him with hate, she thought to herself
that if she were a man, she'd beat his ass on the spot.

Junebug continued talking shit until he felt his point

had been made. Peanut sat in silence, listening. As he rested his hand on the wall cabinet, she saw it move. He felt it. Leaping up from her spot, she hollered "Bingo!" in a deep voice. Moving with the quickness, Peanut began pushing and pulling on the cabinet.

"The shit's behind this wall," she growled. "It moved!"

"Girl, ain't nothin moved," Junebug lied. "You trippin."

"Man, are you gonna help? Because if you ain't, get out of my way."

Peanut slightly lifted the cabinet. Peering behind the crack, she spotted Big Ed's stash. Junebug took a look and felt the lump return to his throat.

"Push it up, Junebug," Peanut demanded.

Junebug lifted the unit from its hinges and carefully placed it on the floor. When he turned around, Peanut was gone. A second later she returned with a giant duffel bag and began placing the dope, money, and guns inside it.

"OK, put the cabinet back," she said.

Junebug did as told. Once the mission was complete, she scooped up the duffel and walked out, double-checking to make certain everything was in place. Turning out the lights and closing the door, they hopped in her bucket and rolled.

18
QUESTIONS, BUT NO ANSWERS

The homicide office housed three interrogation rooms, two for suspects, the third for witnesses. Each room was tiny, consisting of one small table with three chairs. Bolted to the tables in the suspects' rooms were handcuffs. The witness room did not display that luxury.

Since Rodney occupied one suspect room, Big Ed was led to the other, with Leroy taken to the witness room, where Hernandez uncuffed one arm only to snap the cuff on his chair. The detectives knew they couldn't play good cop/bad cop with any of these guys because they were all hardened criminals and would not be frightened. Johnson and Hernandez would have to play it straight, hoping that once they had each man's account of the deadly evening Silky was murdered, they could sift through the stories, then separate truth from lies.

It was a common police tactic to get each man to in-

criminate their accomplices while proclaiming that all
they did was serve as a lookout. The criminals were unaware that in each case they would state similar facts,
which the police would piece together like a jigsaw puzzle.

"Let's question Gates first," Johnson said to his partner.

Rodney heard the key being inserted into the doorknob
and awoke from a restless sleep. He had lined up all three
chairs in a row to create a makeshift bed. His lip was
swollen, hair nappy, face ashen, breath hot, and dried-up
saliva lined the corners of his mouth, creating an ugly-
looking goatee.

"OK, Gates," Johnson started, "here's what we know.
You and the Tatum boys all rode in the limo—by the way,
we have those guys in custody giving their statements
right now." Johnson paused to let his comments fully
sink into Rodney's brain. "The driver has identified you
and it'll only be a matter of time before he does the same
to your homeboys."

"I'ont know what you talkin 'bout," Rodney deadpanned.

"I think you do," Johnson continued. "You guys wanted
to teach Silky a lesson for thinking he could take over
the empire, so you coerced the limo driver into giving up
the ride, followed Silky, then when the timing was right,
killed him. Sound familiar?"

"Hell naw," Rodney whispered, smiling.

"OK, you tell me then."

"Tell you what?"

"What happened the night of Big Ed's coming-home party."

"Awight," Rod sighed, "I went to the party but I drove Big Ed's Mercedes. I'ont know how somebody could identify me in a limo 'cause dat just didn't happen—ah wadn't nowhere near no limo."

"So you're saying you didn't ride in the limousine?"

"Dass what ah'm sayin 'cause dat's how it was."

"If you were in Big Ed's car, then where was he?"

"In da limo."

"Where was Leroy?" Johnson pressed forward.

"I'ont know." Rodney scratched his nappy head. "Ah didn't see Leroy."

"How did Big Ed get his car back from you?"

"He picked it up da next day outside mah crib."

"So you gave him the keys?"

"Naw, he used his spare."

"Basically you want us to believe that you know nothing about Silky's murder?" Johnson's voice rose slightly.

"Man, I'ont give a shit what you ba-leave—ah just tole you what went down wit me, an dass all ah'm sayin."

Rodney rested his head on the table and closed his eyes, faking sleep. Johnson, realizing that he would answer no more questions, nodded to Hernandez, who sat writing at a furious pace. Hernandez turned off the recorder and the two of them exited the room.

"That lying sonofabitch." Hernandez's words dripped with venom.

"Manny, now how do you know his mother is a bitch?"

"Because she had that asshole," Hernandez answered.

Johnson laughed at his partner's response. Not because it was funny; more to the point, he knew Rodney was lying through his gold-plated teeth. It was rare that Nathan Johnson laughed at any comment made by Manny Hernandez directed at blacks. The twosome headed for Leroy's room when suddenly the intercom blared out that a murder had been committed at the waterfront. Since they were the only homicide detectives on duty, they had to respond. Johnson grabbed his jacket and headed for the door, but before he could reach it, it swung open. Derrick Boston and Maria Jimenez strode in to begin their shift.

"Great timing, guys," Johnson said, "now you two get the case."

"What's going down, sir?" Maria asked.

"A call just went out about a 187 at Estuary Park. Since we're in the middle of interviewing suspects, you guys get this one."

"On our way," said Derrick.

He and Maria turned on their heels and left just as quickly as they had arrived. Johnson and Hernandez hung their jackets up again and went to question Leroy. They would save Big Ed for last.

The twosome entered Leroy's interrogation room and immediately noticed the swinging Venetian blinds. They knew he had witnessed their conversation with Derrick and Maria. Whereas the interrogation rooms were windowless, providing only a peephole in the door, the witness room was a converted office with windows on two sides covered by dirty blinds.

"Yaw got moe problems, huh?" grinned Leroy.

"Nothing we can't handle," Johnson answered.

"Don't sound like dat ta me!"

"Look punk...!" Hernandez yelled.

"Ah got yo punk hangin low!" Leroy yelled back.

"Alright Leroy," Johnson boomed, "tell me what happened the night Silky was murdered."

"Who?"

"Duane Johnson—you call him Silky."

"I'ont know nobody named Silky."

"How did you get home from your brother's party?"

"Man, ah was so drunk ah cain't even 'member dat far back."

Hernandez shut off the recorder and jerked Leroy's chair around, grabbing him by the collar of his shirt. The two men were face to face, staring daggers into each other's eyes.

"Listen, you ass, you think you're funny, don't you?"

"Mah momma always said ah coulda been a comedian."

"We should've let Boston beat the crap out of your sorry ass."

"Yeah right, his ass didn't wont no moe uh dis—you seen his face, didn't you?"

Johnson, realizing that this entire episode had turned what should have been an interrogation into a hate meeting between Manny and Leroy, grabbed his partner by the sleeve and escorted him out of the room. Leroy sat smiling as the detectives closed the door. As soon as it slammed shut, he used his free arm to peep through the blinds. Hernandez saw him looking and gave him a finger.

"Manny, you can't let this guy get to you," Johnson told his partner.

"I know, Nate, but I'd like nothing better than to wipe that silly grin off his face."

"Well, at least we have a witness who'll testify that all three men were in the limousine," Johnson stated. "You hungry?"

"Starving," Hernandez replied.

"Good, let's go eat, then question Big Ed when we get back."

"Sounds like a plan."

Hernandez and Johnson walked down the block to their favorite eatery, Mexicali Rose. Engaging in small talk while dipping chips into salsa, they waited for their meals, which arrived in five minutes flat. As was their custom, they ate in silence.

THE
PROFESSIONAL

The black stretch limousine glided down Hegenberger Road towards the airport. Traffic was heavy and slow due to the fact that the street was slick from an earlier downpour of rain. The nervous driver cautiously followed instructions given by the passenger; he couldn't afford to screw this job up.

"OK," Jason spoke, "turn on your wiper blades and set the timer on the first level. That way the blades will knock off the mist every thirty seconds."

"Got it."

"Now when we get to the airport, our passenger will be an older black guy wearing a tuxedo. He'll also have a cane and should be in front of Southwest Airlines because he's some high roller from Vegas."

"Got it," said Tony.

Anthony Blake, or "Tony" as he chose to be called, was

developing a strong dislike for his white trainer. The dude didn't know what he was doing, treating Tony like an idiot. He would be glad when training was over so he could chauffeur alone.

Tony could best be described as a loser. Floating through life on mother wit and his good looks, he'd blown several quality jobs because of stupidity. The reasons varied from quitting in order to "find himself" to calling in sick the day after receiving his first paycheck. No matter what, Tony Blake always found a way to lose a job. He felt like this one would be a perfect fit because it allowed him interaction with people who not only had money, but social status too.

Standing six feet tall on a muscular two-hundred-and-twenty-pound frame, Tony Blake was handsome. He had a lean angular face with skin smoother than a baby's butt, short one-inch natural, pearl-white teeth, and long thick eyelashes.

Tony drove to the airport envisioning himself charming the panties off some rich broad, then letting her take care of him. He didn't care that their passenger tonight was an old dude because he knew sooner or later females would occupy the back seat.

"There he is!" shouted Jason.

"Where?" Tony asked, dream interrupted.

"Right there. Pull over and remember to address him as 'Sir' all night."

"Yeah," Tony said sourly as he got out. "Hello sir," he greeted the passenger.

"Hello young man," the old guy responded.

"Mr. Jones, right?"

"That's correct."

"My name is Tony and I'll be your driver for the evening. Are there any special requests?"

"Well, now that you inquire, yes, there is."

"What's that, sir?"

"I'm starving, so if it's not much to ask, could we stop at a burger joint and get a bite to eat?"

"No problem," Tony said, "where would you like to go?"

"I don't know—you see, I'm not from these parts."

"Well, since your destination is in the Square, I know the perfect place. Do you have any luggage?"

"Not really, just this overnight bag." The old guy leaned close to Tony and whispered, "I call this a one-night stand."

"Oh, a booty call, huh?" Tony grinned.

"That's what you young folks call it; to me it's a night out with a beautiful young woman whose husband is out of town."

"So I have the luxury of driving around an OG tonight, huh?"

Before the man could respond, Jason, who thought Tony was taking too long, hopped out of the vehicle and proceeded to interrupt what had been light-hearted banter between the two black men.

"Hello sir, my name is Jason Collins and I'm Tony's instructor. This is his first assignment so he's still a little rough around the edges. Is everything alright?"

"It's fine," said Mr. Jones.

"Good enough—are you ready to go?"

"Yes."

"OK, Tony," Jason snapped his finger, "put his bag in the trunk."

"No need," said Jones. "This bag never leaves my sight."

"As you wish, sir."

Jason re-entered the limo, failing to see the eye Tony gave the old man, who nodded his head, letting Tony know that he understood. Jones was decked out in a black tux with red cummerbund and bowtie. His matching red hanky was neatly folded and poking out from his jacket pocket. He also wore a long black trench coat, top hat with the band and feather both red, and expensive Italian shoes. Thick salt-and-pepper sideburns connected to a mustache and goatee were all trimmed and neat. The walking cane his hand rested on was black with a cobra head on top. Folding it into three even parts, he snapped its latch, which held it in place.

Tony stood at the open back door smiling as Mr. Jones took his time entering the vehicle. Once he joined Jason in the front, Tony informed him of the special request.

"Dressed like that and he wants a burger?" Jason couldn't believe it.

"That's what he wants," Tony answered.

"Well, if that don't beat all!" Jason laughed to himself.

Tony cruised past the airport terminals to Hegenberger Road, thinking about how sweet it would be to kick Jason's ass. Grinning to himself, he got on 880 and rolled downtown. Floating into an empty lot at 4th & Broadway, he parked then turned on the intercom.

"Mr. Jones, Nation's is right next door and their food

is on hits—what would you like, sir?"

"I'd like you to roll down this glass separating us so we can converse man to man." Tony did as instructed. "Now all I want is a cheeseburger, fries, and chocolate shake." Jones handed Tony a hundred-dollar bill before whispering, "Keep the change."

Tony's face lit up like a Christmas tree while Jason jealously looked on, his brain already calculating how much his "half" would be. Tony bounced from the ride sporting his tux and chauffeur hat like a macaroni prince. Jason wracked his brain trying to think of something to say to the old guy but came up empty.

"You're doing a fine job training him," Jones said, breaking the ice.

"Thank you, sir," Jason responded. "He'll be alright."

"With you as his instructor he'll be excellent."

Ten minutes later Tony returned with the food to find Jason and Mr. Jones engaged in conversation as if they were longtime friends.

"That peckawood tryin ta ease in on my play," he thought to himself. "Here you go, Mr. Jones," Tony said as he handed him the food.

" 'Sir,' Tony—address him as 'Sir'," admonished Jason while smiling at Jones.

"Listen to the man, son," Jones told Tony, "he's training you right."

"Yes sir." Tony's tone was dry.

"Now I still have an hour to kill, so do you guys know of a location where I can eat in peace, preferably a waterfront?"

"The Estuary," Jason spoke up.

"Good, take me there."

Tony started the engine and cruised to the Estuary highly upset. He was quiet as a mouse while Jason and the old man chatted away. Pulling the stretch limo to a halt by the waterfront, Tony sat behind the wheel steaming.

There were a few cars in the lot with young lovers making out. Trucks and sport utility vehicles sat empty with trailer hitches minus the boats they towed. Placing his meal on the table provided, Jones spoke to Tony.

"Young man," he said, "could I trouble you for a minute and get you to dump this down the restroom toilet?"

Jason and Tony both turned around to see what the old man wanted, with Jason forcing himself not to laugh out loud. Jones held up a plastic container filled with urine. It was the same kind that wheelchair-bound or cancer patients used.

"Use your gloves," Jason smiled wickedly at Tony.

Tony accepted the container from Jones and exited the vehicle to the restroom. The minute his door shut, Jones spoke to Jason, "That young man still has a lot to learn about customer service."

"Don't worry, Mr. Jones, I'll whip him into shape," Jason boasted.

"Let me tell you something."

Jones leaned up in his seat while Jason tilted his head back. The moment he did, Jones cupped a hand over his mouth and slit his throat from ear to ear with a very large hunting knife. Jason's eyes bulged enormously large while his hands furiously attempted to pull the gloved hand of Mr. Jones away from his lips.

Releasing his grip, Jones grabbed his cane, travel bag, and food, then opened the door, casually strolling to a silver Mercedes parked between two trucks. Starting the engine, he rolled away from the Estuary to Jack London Square.

Tony returned from the restroom still angry at Jones and Jason. Now he didn't give a damn about the ninety-four-dollar tip because he felt as though he had been dissed, which is the number-one offense you can commit on a young black man.

"Fuck bofe uh dose muafuckas," he grumbled to himself while opening the door. The sight his eyes rested on caused him to drop the container and scream for help. Jason's body sat upright in the passenger seat with blood gurgling from his neck. He was dead as a doorknob.

People slowly emerged from their autos gasping at the sight while Tony became animated in his actions. First he checked the back seat, finding it empty, then he spun around in a few circles crying his eyes out. Not only was Jason dead, Jones was kidnapped, he thought.

Dialing 911 on his cell phone, he shouted into the receiver, informing the dispatcher of his predicament. Two minutes later, squad cars along with paramedics arrived on the scene. Since Jason was dead, the area was cordoned off with yellow tape and everyone questioned.

Tony went to the station with beat cops, where they had him pore over mug shot photos searching for Mr. Jones. This task would take all night. After he called

Angelo Tortellini and informed him of the evening's events, Tony hung up the phone dejected. He knew he'd be fired.

"Mission accomplished," said Sweetpea, who immediately hung up his untraceable cell phone. Heading to the back of his Benz, he opened the trunk then peeled off his hat, gloves, fake sideburns, mustache, and goatee, which he placed carefully into a shopping bag.

Now clean-shaven, he removed his coat, jacket, bow tie, shirt, and cummerbund, displaying a fly blue rayon shirt with crimson streaks. Ripping off the tuxedo slacks in the same manner a hoopster does their warm-up sweats, Sweetpea was now decked out in blue.

Casually removing his shoes, he lifted a pair of navy-blue loafers from the trunk then headed for the bright lights of the Square. Stopping at a dumpster, he tossed the two bags of clothing plus his fast food inside, then went for a real meal.

Sweetpea was an assassin for hire and the best in the business because he never got caught. The man was a pro's pro. Satisfied with his night's work, he strode into the Ark to enjoy a delicious steak and lobster meal.

Looking nothing like the man Tony would describe to Five-O, he smiled at his own cleverness. Besides, if he felt that Tony was a threat, Tony would be dead now too. Since the young dude was hip, Sweetpea chose to let him live another day.

THE NIGHTMARE
CONTINUES

Boston and Jimenez returned to headquarters, heading for the lineup room where Tony pored over mug shots. Having browsed through several stacks of books, he still came up empty. Even if he had spotted Mr. Jones, he would not have told because he seemed to understand that the man let him live on purpose.

Speaking quietly to the officers guarding Tony, Boston learned that he would be useless in identifying the suspect. Boston made a call to have a sketch artist draw a mug shot of the character based on Tony's description. That done, he and his partner headed for homicide to relay the bad news to Johnson and Hernandez.

The two detectives were returning from the restaurant stuffed and satisfied. Now they would question Big Ed, anticipating that he would be just as vague as Rodney and Leroy. The two stepped it up to the entry door on Washington Street, which was nearest their office.

"Hey Sarge," Boston said blandly to Johnson as he inserted the key into the door lock.

"You guys look like you saw a ghost," Johnson stated.

"Worse than that," Boston answered as they all went inside, "the victim was none other than our ace witness, Jason Collins."

"Dammit!" Hernandez flung his hands upwards. "The nightmare continues!"

Hernandez saw the blinds in Leroy's room shake, which meant one thing—he'd witnessed the entire conversation.

"Nosey sonofabitch!" Hernandez screamed while bulling his way to Leroy's room.

"Wait amigo." Johnson calmly blocked his path. "Not now."

Hernandez was furious—he would have liked nothing better than to go inside that room and beat the living hell out of Leroy. Before he could respond to Johnson, there was a knock at the door. Boston opened it to a smiling Samuel Waterman.

"All present and accounted for," Waterman jived as he entered the office.

"Sam, how you doing?" Johnson asked.

"I'm good, Nathan," he responded. "Manuel?"

"Hey amigo, what brings you here?" Manny returned.

Sam Waterman was sole owner of Precious Bonds. A dapper-looking guy at the tender age of seventy, his youthfulness, zest for life, and money kept him young. He stood six-feet-two on a slender hundred-and-eighty-pound frame. Possessing a flair for haberdashery, Sam was always suited and booted.

Today he wore a black-and-white pinstripe suit, alligator shoes to match, white pimp socks, striped necktie, and black derby with white band and red feather. Gold saturated his wrists and fingers, along with a sparkling diamond in his earlobe.

As was his custom, he greeted everyone by their full first name and would beat around the bush until he had gathered the information he desired. Johnson knew Sam well and surmised that this wasn't a social visit. Since they had arrested Big Ed at his place of business, somehow Waterman had a stake in the mess. Johnson figured that money was the connecting factor because Sam was about money, plain and simple.

"Young lady, I don't think we've had the pleasure...." Sam extended his hand to Maria's.

"Maria Jimenez." She held out hers, and he kissed the back while lifting his brim. Maria grinned.

"Young man?"

"Derrick Boston."

"Just call me Sam, Derrick." They shook.

"I believe my partner asked what brings you here?" Johnson smiled.

"Yes, he did, Nathan, but my mom—may she rest in peace—always told me that if I didn't sleep with a woman, to greet her." He stared at Maria, who smiled back.

"OK, now that that's over...." Nate continued.

"Well Nathan, you arrested someone in my office today and since I'm not his attorney, I'm not sure if it's my place to ask...."

"Ask what?" Johnson interrupted.

"What are the charges?" Waterman toyed with his brim.

"Suspicion of murder." Johnson was direct.

"Has bail been set?"

"Not yet, Sam—why?"

"Just curious, Nathan—you know I'm always on my P's & Q's."

"Sam? Now how long have we known each other? Twenty-five years?"

"More or less," Waterman smiled.

"Well, based on that, good buddy, I know you got some sort of angle in this mess. If you didn't, you wouldn't be here. Give it to me straight, Sam."

Boston, Jimenez, and Hernandez, who'd up to now watched the banter between the two longtime buddies with amusement, all burst out laughing. So did Sam and Nate.

"Well, Nathan"—Sam scratched his bald head—"the young man left a deposit, but before he could tell us what the money was to be used for, he was arrested."

"He probably wanted to post bail for his flunkeys."

"You mean there are others?" Sam had his info.

"Yes," Johnson said, "his brother and top lieutenant."

"If I'm not being too nosey, could you tell me the gentleman's name?"

"Absolutely—one Edward Jerome Tatum."

"Oh, Edward." Sam wasn't surprised. "One of my best customers. Well, I hate to cut such a wonderful visit short, but I do have a business to run."

"We'll let you know when bail is set, Sam," Johnson said.

"Nathan, your kindness will never be forgotten. Young lady"—he kissed Maria's hand again as she cheesed, "Gentlemen."

Waterman shook Derrick and Manny's hands, cocked his brim on his dome, and strutted out like a peacock.

"Now that's a character!" Maria laughed.

"Yes, Maria," Johnson boomed, "but also a very smart man."

"What now, Nate?" Hernandez asked.

"We have no choice but to let these three clowns loose."

Hernandez let out a long sigh as Johnson opened each door, releasing the prisoners. Big Ed, Rodney, and Leroy grinned at each other, knowing that they were off the hook. Rodney and Leroy looked at Big Ed with admiration, knowing that he was the reason they were free.

Leroy didn't know how he'd accomplished this feat but figured that phone call he made at the cookhouse had something to do with it. Once they signed out for their belongings, Big Ed led them to Precious Bonds.

Rodney and Leroy waited outside while Big Ed went in to conduct his business. When he exited the office, he shook hands with a fly-looking old guy then instructed his brother and henchman to ride in the back seat while he got into the front of a taxicab.

The ride back to Leroy's crib was a silent one, with each man absorbed in his own personal thoughts. They exited the taxi with Big Ed peeling off a c-note and telling the surprised driver to keep the change. Entering Leroy's funky, ramshackle apartment, the three men plopped down on the sofa and loveseat. It was good to be free—they would pay some dopefiends to patch up the place later.

DOUBLE-CROSSED

Peanut hooked a U-turn and sped down Second, making a right on D Street. Streaking past San Clemente Park and turning left on Maud, she decreased her speed. Three minutes later, she slowly rolled through the gates into Don Castro Regional Park.

Cruising past the entrance booth—empty since it was a weekday—she rolled past the lake, playfield, swimming pool, and campsites, parking on the second tier near the hiking trails. Junebug was still antsy, which Peanut didn't like.

"Junebug, why you so fidgety?"

"Ain't nobody fidgety—we just should'na done that."

"Yes we should have!" She was proud. "Now let's see what we got."

Peanut unzipped the duffel bag, screaming at the sight her eyes rested on. She happily began pulling out stacks of cash. When she looked up to ask her accomplice why he was so quiet, her mug was introduced to a thundering right hand.

Junebug began pummeling Peanut's face into a bloody mess, with her helpless to stop the onslaught. Opening the door, she fell out of the vehicle then got up, attempting to run. That ploy was unsuccessful because since the girl was punch-drunk, she stumbled a few steps before falling face-first to the pavement.

"Junebug, what you doin?" she cried.

"Bitch, ah tole you ah ain't gone have nuttin to do wit dis shit!" he yelled while rapidly approaching.

Remembering the gun she had secretly stuffed into the small of her back, she lifted it from its hiding place. Too late: Junebug stomped violently on her wrist, causing the gun to fall harmlessly on the cement. Picking it up, he held it point-blank to her chest and fired.

Peanut's body rose and fell upon impact of the bullet before going limp. Junebug got up, dragged her body by the shoulders into the weeds and bushes, then hopped in her hoopty and sped off.

His mind raced a mile a minute. He originally intended to go to Crystal's home but upon second thought headed to Leroy's. Knocking on the door, he was greeted by a smiling Rodney. Ignoring him, he flung the duffel bag to the floor, telling a somber-looking Big Ed, "Here's yo shit, man."

"What shit?" Big Ed perked up from the sofa.

"Da shit dat bitch tried ta steal from you—ah stopped her ass, dough."

"Man, what you talkin 'bout?" Big Ed asked while opening the bag.

"Ah'm talkin 'bout Crystal's sister Peanut!" Junebug screamed. "Well, her real name is Melody an dat's da bitch ah tole you Silky never wanted me ta know about. Now check dis: da bitch followed you to yo mama's crib and when ah took her sistah da cah, she was already dare waitin foe me. Said she followed you an saw you get sumptin from da garage—she was sho you got either money, dope, or both."

"So you knowed who da bitch was all da time?" Big Ed arched his brow.

"Dude, ah tole you ah didn't know da bitch, but ah did see her at Silky's mama's house after da funeral."

"Why you go ride with her den?!" Big Ed shouted.

"'Cause if she was gone try an rob you, man, ah was gone make sho dat didn't happen. Now thank"—Junebug tapped his temple—"if ah didn't go along wit da bitch's program, yo ass broke. Tole you ah'm yo boy—what is it gone take fa you ta trust me?"

Big Ed pondered the news Junebug had just relayed. He had many questions running through his brain because this entire sequence of events didn't add up. Checking his loot, he quietly asked, "How did she get in mah momma's garage?"

"She saw yo key in da cup holder and hid it," he lied.

"How she find mah shit?" he toyed with a gun.

"She searched around, man." Junebug watched the pistol.

"Crystal in on it?"

"I'ont know, man, but dey is sistahs."

"Where da bitch now?"

"I bumped her off."

"Anybody see you?" His eyes bore a hole through Junebug's.

"Naw, dude, it was clean as a whistle."

"What about the body, her purse, car...?"

"Her body is hid in some bushes, purse in da bag, cah right outside."

"OUTSIDE!" Big Ed jumped to his feet, slugging Junebug in the mouth. "Dumb muthafucka!" he yelled. "Dass gone brang da police right heah!"

Big Ed kicked Junebug savagely in the ribs, causing him to double over in pain, then elbowed him on the back of the neck. Junebug sprawled out on the dirty carpet, instantly begging forgiveness. Big Ed grabbed a handful of permed hair, looked Junebug directly in the eye, then released a wicked right to the temple that knocked Junebug out cold.

"Rod, Leroy, listen up, yaw—dis shit impotant," he whispered. "Rod, you drive dat hoe's cah ta Arroyo Park and leave it—leave da does unlocked an da key in da ignition. Den yaw come back heah."

"What about him?" asked Rodney, pointing at Junebug.

"DON'T WORRY 'BOUT HIM!" Big Ed hollered. "Juss do what ah tell ya!"

Rodney and Leroy rushed out the door like flies chasing shit. All three men felt dirty and needed baths, but that would have to wait. Big Ed went into the kitchen and retrieved a roll of duct tape from a utility drawer.

Returning to the living room, he taped Junebug's eyes, mouth, nose, wrists, and ankles tighter than a drum. Folding up the body in a fetal position, he wrapped tape around Junebug's knees and neck several times before emptying a storage trunk and shoving the limp figure inside.

Thinking twice, he dumped the body back onto the floor then rolled it into a garbage bag, tying it up before returning it to the trunk. Hoisting the trunk onto his shoulders, he gingerly marched out of the apartment and down the steps, balancing it like a tightrope artist would a pole for leverage.

Next, Big Ed opened the lift gate to his monster truck, which had been parked at Leroy's place, and shoved the chest inside. Running back up the stairs, he grabbed his duffel bag and left. Stopping at a first-floor unit, he pounded on the door. A fine-shaped woman answered with her hands on her hips. She was wearing nothing but a see-through negligee.

Robin McGee was one of Big Ed's many women and would do anything he asked. They had known each other since grade school and been lovers since their teen years. She was built like a track star with tree-trunk thighs, muscular legs, and a nice-looking booty. The girl had a small waist, baseball-sized tits, and a cute face. Although she had three kids by three different men and was a welfare recipient her entire adult life, she lived well thanks to Big Ed's "gifts."

Since she would sneak around on her boyfriends to have sex with Big Ed whenever he wanted, he knew she could be trusted. Besides, she reminded him every chance she got that he should have chosen her instead of Shirley.

"What's up, baby?" she asked.

"Robin, I need a favor," Big Ed said as he hurried past her, closing the door.

"What is it, honey?" She showed concern.

"I need you to guard this bag with your life."

"You know I'll do anything for you."

Reaching into the duffel bag, he tossed her two bundles of money.

"Dass fa yo trouble," he said.

"No trouble, baby—wanna make love?"

"Ain't got no time," he answered, "but when ah get back, be ready."

Big Ed kissed her savagely while feeling her up and down, then walked out. Robin sat on her sofa and began counting the money he'd given her. Realizing she had twenty thousand dollars, she had a powerful orgasm.

As Big Ed slid into his Bronco, Leroy and Rodney returned, joining him.

"Heah." Leroy handed his brother a gun.

"Where did this come from?" Big Ed was surprised.

"We found it in da hoopty."

"See, dat dumb muthafucka didn't even hide the gun."

Big Ed went to the back, opened the storage cabinet, and casually placed the pistol inside next to Junebug's dead body. Driving to the San Leandro Marina, he found a secluded spot and backed into a stall.

The three men got out and lifted the storage locker from the trunk of the Bronco. Filling it with several loose rocks in order to weigh it down, they hoisted it into the water. As it slowly submerged into the depths of the ocean, Big Ed contemplated his next move. He didn't know if anyone else was aware of his secret hiding spot at his mom's crib, so he wasn't sure if he could keep his property there anymore. He also needed to get with Crystal in order to find out how much or what she knew.

"Whatup now, boss?" Rodney asked.

"Let's go to mah so-called bitch's house."

Jumping inside, the deadly trio headed for Crystal's pad in order to find out what she knew. If she knew too much, Big Ed would kill her.

Rolling up to the Parkside Terrace, Big Ed parked on the street at the rear of the building. The threesome exited the vehicle and entered from the back gate. Crystal was gone but had left Big Ed a note on the kitchen counter.

> Baby,
> I had to make a run to Highland's to see my sister—don't know when I'll be back. If you need me, just call my cellular and leave a message. I'll check periodically.
> LOVE,
> Crystal

"She don't know nuttin," Big Ed said to Leroy.

"Why you say dat, dog?" questioned his brother while helping himself to a shot of brandy.

"Look at da note, fool!" he shouted.

While Leroy and Rodney helped themselves to food and drink, Big Ed grabbed the remote control off the coffee table and turned on the television. Turning to channel eight, which was a special feature channel that displayed the front entrance to Crystal's building, he watched as the usual assortment of tenants and mail delivery personnel went about their daily routine.

Ten minutes elapsed and Big Ed was bored to death. With his brain thinking a zillion miles a minute, he rose up off the sofa. Before he could click off the remote control, something caught his eye. Two uniformed officers along with Hernandez were waiting at the front door, then the building manager wandered through the lobby. Big Ed knew they were on to him.

"Let's raise," he said to Leroy and Rod, "take yo shit wit you."

Leroy and Rodney did as told, leaving the remaining portions of grub on the table but taking their drinks with them. Just as they got to the door leading to the street, Big Ed blurted out, "Yaw wait foe me outside—ah fa-got sumptin."

Rodney and Leroy headed out the gate while Big Ed went back to the condo.

22
FRESH LEAD

Johnson returned from CID to the homicide office where Hernandez, Boston, and Jimenez waited patiently. He'd requested that undercover surveillance be placed on the three hoods he was forced to release.

"What's our next move, Nate?" Hernandez inquired.

"Derrick, you and Maria go back and question the limousine driver, then head to their office and try to find out the name of the person who rented the car, who paid the bill, or anything else you can dig up."

"You got it," Boston said as he and his partner rose up out of their chairs.

"Manny, first we'll go have another chat with Silky's girlfriend...."

"That would be Ms. Boudreaux," Hernandez said while flipping through his notepad.

"Yes," Johnson answered, "then we'll visit the elderly

couple before they leave town."

"The Montagues," Hernandez supplied.

"Correct again, amigo," Johnson confirmed. "If you guys find out anything relevant or vice versa, we'll contact each other by cell phone. If not, let's meet here in three hours."

Plan in motion, the four detectives headed out the door, with Boston and Jimenez making their way to Tony, who was almost finished with the mug shot albums. Johnson and Hernandez hopped in their service vehicle and took 580 to Melody's crib.

Upon finding no one home, they left a calling card in the door then sped off towards the Hyatt Regency. As they crossed the intersection of 73rd & East 14th, Hernandez's cell phone rang.

The call was from an excited Derrick Boston, telling them to meet him at Highland Hospital's intensive care unit immediately. Hernandez relayed the message to his partner, who hit 880 to 23rd. Red light flashing on the dashboard, Johnson pulled up in the hospital's emergency parking lot four minutes later.

Boston and Jimenez were already there, and upon seeing the two senior detectives, filled them in on what was going down. The foursome entered the hospital and made a beeline to intensive care.

23
POSITIVE ID

The ambulance sped down 580 towards the trauma center at Highland Hospital with lights flashing and sirens at full blast. Inside, the EMTs furiously attempted to revive the patient. They also worked at a rapid pace to stop the bleeding.

Since the young black woman possessed no identification, she was tentatively labeled "Jane Doe" but that didn't matter to the crew. A human being's life hung in the balance, so they didn't care what her name was or how she'd pay her medical bill.

The red and white van rolled into the emergency stall with the paramedics gently lifting the gurney out and placing it on the asphalt. Rushing it into the operating room where trained staff waited to perform surgery, the three technicians took refuge in the hallway consoling one another.

Doctors began performing their craft while police officers assigned to the trauma center questioned the ambulance staff. They wanted to know from where the body was retrieved, any witnesses, identification, what law enforcement agency handled the initial report, and any additional information they could provide.

Three hours later the operating team members slowly marched out of the room. As they hugged and shook hands with one another, it was obvious to all viewing that a life had been saved. The chief surgeon strolled out wiping his brow with a paper towel while lowering his facemask, letting it dangle from his neck.

The EMTs had long since vacated the premises to answer more calls. They would be back later to find out the status of the lady whose life they tried to prolong. The officers waited patiently for the surgeon, who approached them immediately.

Michael Guillory was a third-generation doctor following in his dad and grandfather's footsteps. Strikingly handsome, he stood six-foot-three on a chiseled two-hundred-and-forty-pound frame. Blond and blue-eyed, he resembled a surfer or beach volleyball star. As he walked over to the rookie cops assigned hospital duty, the doctor let out a sigh of relief while shaking their hands and pulling off the cap that held his hair in place.

John Martin and Eric Prevost, the two cops, both had less than a year's service since graduating from the academy. They considered this assignment a coup because it meant they did not have to go through the daily grind of patrol duty, which consisted of wrestling with, shooting at, and chasing down suspects through backyards and blind alleyways.

"Well fellas, she's gonna make it," Dr. Guillory said. "Had the bullet landed an inch to either side, she would be dead."

"She must have an angel looking out for her, huh, Doc?" said Prevost, the bulkier of the two officers.

"I'll say." The doctor wiped his brow. "Any idea who she is?"

"We're checking dental charts and fingerprints—we should have a positive ID by nightfall."

Doctor Guillory chatted with the two uniformed officers for a few more minutes before heading off to yet another operation. They would shoot the breeze while standing guard, hoping the lady would be identified on their shift.

* * *

Peaches wandered around the hospital aimlessly, tugging her IV unit. Since her rape, which lasted the better part of two days and involved at least a dozen different men, she'd uttered nary a word to hospital staff. The girl was traumatized severely.

As she walked, she appeared to be in a trance, not caring that her ass was showing through the open gap in the back of her gown. Most of the male doctors and nurses appeared to ignore her, while secretly lusting the black woman with the nappy head, ugly mug, but movie-star figure. Many in the intensive care unit considered her to be 151 (crazy) yet harmless.

Seeing a familiar face, Peaches stopped in her tracks then entered the room and sat down. Peanut lay strapped to her bed with tubes attached to her nostrils, mouth, and veins. She was unconscious and unaware of her visitor due to the heavy doses of painkillers injected in her system.

Guadalupe Sanchez walked briskly through the corridors of the hospital looking for her patient. "Lupe" hated it when her mental patients got lost because there was no telling where they would wind up, and since this particular woman could not talk, the task of finding her increased threefold. A short Latina with a butterball figure and flaming red hair, Lupe silently cursed under her breath as her forehead began to perspire.

"There you are," she smiled upon spotting Peaches. "Come on honey, we have to go back now." She reached for her arm.

"I know her," Peaches whispered, jerking her arm away.

"You wait right here," a stunned Lupe told Peaches.

Glancing at the medical chart, she read where Peanut was listed as Jane Doe, so Lupe decided to inform her boss not only of their patient's ability to speak, but also the fact that she could identify a gunshot victim. Turning on her heels, Lupe almost ran over Dr. Guillory, who'd just sewn up a stabbing victim.

"Doctor," she gasped, "I have some incredible news!"

"Calm down, nurse," Guillory said. "Now, what is it?"

"I have a patient in this room who we thought could not talk, but now I know she can."

"Good for you," the doctor said.

"Wait, there's more." She spoke rapidly. "Not only can

she talk, she claims to know the name of your mystery gunshot victim."

"Let's question her."

They hurried into the room, with everyone at the nurses' station watching with more than a passing interest.

"Good afternoon, ma'am," the doctor greeted Peaches.

"Hello," Peaches responded.

"The nurse tells me you can identify my patient."

"She's my friend—her name is Melody Boudreaux."

"Do you know any of her relatives?"

"She has a sister named Crystal. Hayes I believe is her last name."

"Anyone else?"

"Not that I know of."

Dr. Guillory exited the room with Lupe right on his heels. "Nurse," he spoke, "take her back to the mental ward, and I'll track down her sister. I'll also tell the police what we have. We may be onto something here."

"Yes sir."

"Excellent work, Lupe—you deserve a raise."

Guadalupe's chest swelled with pride from the doctor's statement because she knew she would be receiving kudos from all of her co-workers for a job well done. Doctor Guillory placed a call to Five-O informing them that he had a name for their Jane Doe patient. After giving Derrick Boston the particulars, he waited for Oaktown's finest to arrive.

Derrick smiled at Maria, then called Johnson, telling him to meet them at Highland's emergency entrance pronto.

THE EYES HAVE IT

Foster and McDavid followed the taxicab carrying Big Ed, Leroy, and Rodney to Sunnyside. Thirty minutes later they watched as Junebug ran up the steps and entered.

Roger Foster and Kyle McDavid had worked as an undercover tag team for nearly three years and loved their job. They also enjoyed working with vice as drug buyers because the street-level dealers never knew they were cops. In fact, these two were so good at their job that many in the department didn't even know them. Foster's appearance was straight from the streets. Five-eleven with a full beard and cornrows, he possessed a milk-chocolate complexion and gift for gab.

McDavid, who was five-feet-nine, looked like a poster boy. He was high yellow with a clean-shaven face, curly black hair, and boyish features, making him appear to be no older than twenty-two even though he was almost thirty.

Upon seeing Leroy and Rodney leave in separate cars, one belonging to Junebug, they quickly devised a plan. They'd follow those two for a few minutes and if they split up, the two undercover cops would return to Sunnyside and keep surveillance on Big Ed. If their plan failed, all leads would be lost but it was a risk they didn't mind taking. Three minutes and fourteen blocks later they struck pay dirt. Parking down the block on 81st & Olive, they watched intently as Rodney left what they assumed to be Junebug's car in the lot and sped off with Leroy.

McDavid radioed central dispatch, giving the license plate of the vehicle abandoned at Arroyo Park and requesting that it be towed to the station, while at the wheel Foster followed Leroy back to the apartment.

As the dispatch operator informed them that the car was registered to Melody Boudreaux and had not been reported stolen, they saw Big Ed pull out of the driveway with Rodney and Leroy in the vehicle with him. Foster trailed from a one-block distance. McDavid then placed a call to Johnson.

"Johnson here."

"Sarge, we followed these three to an apartment complex on Sunnyside, then two of them left, abandoning a vehicle at Arroyo Park. It is registered to a Melody Boudreaux."

"Boudreaux," he whispered. "We're at Highland General with her now—she's been shot. What's your location?"

"Traveling east on Bancroft. The suspects appear to be heading out of the city."

"Keep a tail, Kyle, and whatever you do, don't lose 'em."

"Ten-four."

McDavid filled Foster in on the conversation as each man's adrenaline rose three levels. They knew the crooks had made a mistake. Parking amongst the cars at El Torito restaurant on the San Leandro Marina, McDavid lifted his mini-binoculars from the glove box. Upon seeing the three men hoist a chest into the ocean, he told his partner to radio dispatch and request a dive team.

Once again they tailed Big Ed from a one-block distance, with McDavid calling Johnson to inform him of their activities. Even though they had just witnessed what was doubtlessly a crime, the two cops both knew that if they arrested those three on the spot, their days as undercover officers would be history because every criminal in the city would know who they were. That was too much of a risk.

"Call for backup and have them arrested," Johnson boomed through the receiver. "Charge them with attempted murder of Ms. Boudreaux and littering for the chest— we're en route."

"Ten-four, boss," McDavid replied, ending the call then placing another to dispatch.

Following their quarry to the Parkside Terrace, Foster and McDavid watched as Big Ed, Leroy, and Rodney entered the building from an outside door located at the rear of the complex. Five minutes later Johnson and Hernandez rolled up on the set, along with three San Leandro PD squad cars.

After introductions, Hernandez and two of the uniformed cops rode around the block to the front entrance.

Calling the building manager's unit on the security phone, they waited until he waltzed through the lobby to let them in.

Hernandez quickly explained the situation, got the unit number for Crystal's pad, then headed down the hallway with one of the patrol cops. The other one remained posted at the front door.

"You"—Johnson motioned to the beat cop—"drive to the other end of the block, and as soon as the suspects exit the gate, roll up on them."

"Yes sir," he said while re-entering his patrol car.

"Guys"—Johnson spoke to Foster and McDavid—"only reveal your presence if the situation warrants it." They knew he meant if their lives depended on it.

"Ten-four, Sarge," they responded in unison.

Leroy and Rodney walked out of the back door holding their drinks. As they made their way across the street a squad car screeched to a halt behind them. With the siren blaring, the uniformed officer jumped out and trained his gun on them.

Johnson activated his transmitter and warned Hernandez that only two suspects came out. Big Ed was still inside.

"Freeze, you're under arrest!" shouted the officer.

"Arrest for what?" yelled Rodney while raising his hands in the air.

Leroy, realizing it was two of them and only one officer, broke into a full sprint in the opposite direction. Halfway down the block he noticed Johnson heading his way, gun at the ready. Throwing his hands up in exasperation, he stomped violently on the ground.

"Get your hands up where I can see them!" Johnson demanded.

Leroy dove between two cars and pulled out his own gun, which momentarily startled Johnson and created a stand-off. The beat cop, who was just about to handcuff Rodney, watched the drama unfold, which proved to be a serious mistake.

Rodney, on his knees waiting to be cuffed, took advantage of the officer's inattention. Grabbing the man's crotch with one hand and shirt with the other, he lifted the cop like a rag doll and body-slammed him onto the concrete.

Foster and McDavid, who'd watched the entire series of events unfold from the Blazer, knew they had to reveal their identity because fellow officers' lives were at stake. McDavid ran across the street and did a flying tackle on Rodney, who was pummeling the officer's face into a bloody mess. Foster positioned himself behind a car directly across from Leroy and took dead aim.

"Drop it, son—we don't want to shoot you!" Johnson hollered.

"Okay okay, ah'm puttin da gun down, jus tell dis fool don't shoot!" Leroy screamed while eyeballing Foster.

Meanwhile, Hernandez banged on the door of Crystal's apartment shouting, "POLICE, OPEN UP!" With no response, he stepped back then kicked the door so hard it opened and nearly shut again. Before it could close, he and the officer were inside, guns drawn and ready for anything.

Carefully searching the entire unit, Hernandez came

up empty. Checking with the cop at the front door proved fruitless as well.

"Nate, he's not here," Hernandez spoke through his microphone.

"OK Manny, cordon off the building and search every unit—we have these two in custody. I'm coming in."

The next two hours were spent with the officers conducting a thorough search of the entire building and grounds along with the garage, garbage dumpsters, and parked cars. Big Ed was nowhere to be found.

Johnson placed an all-points bulletin out for Big Ed Tatum, which resulted in a massive manhunt throughout the streets of San Leandro. Anyone remotely resembling Big Ed would be stopped, meaning that many law-abiding black citizens were sure to be harassed that day.

FAMILY MATTERS

Horace Boudreaux sat behind his maple-wood desk browsing through applications. Most of the papers only required his signature, since his staff had jotted down notes on each with stickum memos.

Serving as the manager of Wittman, Meyer & Duke mortgage company, Horace's job was like many in upper management—boring. Basically he was just a figurehead, signing off on loans and discussing questionable applications with staff.

Placing the papers neatly on his desk, he rose from his chair and gazed out the high-rise window at the many office workers scurrying back to their jobs from lunch. His job lacked the excitement his brain yearned for, but it did pay well. Horace Boudreaux was a man who craved adventure.

He stood six-one with a salt-and-pepper two-inch afro.

A distinguished-looking fellow with a lean angular build, he had aged gracefully at fifty. Decked out in brown penny loafers with matching socks and slacks, he kept his white business shirts pressed to a crisp and wore a color-coordinated necktie.

Deciding on pasta for lunch, Horace returned to his desk, shut down his computer, then lifted his jacket from the coat rack with intentions of heading for City Center. The door opened before he could reach it as his secretary Harriet rushed up to him.

"Mr. Boudreaux, your sister's been shot!" she gasped.

"Shot?" he questioned. "Which one?"

"Melody," she said. "They have her at Highland in intensive care. I just received the call from Crystal. She said for you to come right away!"

Horace stood there stunned. This was not the sort of excitement he desired. After accepting a hug from Harriet, he rushed to the emergency unit at Highland General. Barging past the sliding plate-glass door, he received directions from the security desk then headed to his sister's room.

Upon entering, he found the place overcrowded. Derrick Boston and Maria Jimenez stood right outside the curtain. Johnson and Hernandez occupied spots in the corner, speaking quietly with Dr. Guillory and Guadalupe. Crystal along with Peaches sat in chairs next to the bed.

"So, what brings you guys here, seeing this is not a murder?" Guillory asked Johnson. They knew each other well.

"We're investigating a case where she was with a guy

when he got killed—matter of fact, we'd just left her home when the call came in for us to come here."

"Horace!" Crystal shouted.

"What happened?" he asked.

"I don't know—she hasn't woken up yet."

At that moment Melody's eyes opened a bit and she peered around the room drowsily, still feeling the effects of the medication. All eyes were on her. Johnson's cell phone rang, so he opened the window, leaned out, then spoke in hushed tones. He knew, along with everyone else, that it was against hospital regulations to use a cell phone while on the premises. As long as his torso remained out the window, he could not be considered inside.

"Try and remember, honey," Horace said. "What happened?"

"OK," Melody said, "I'll try."

"Excuse me," Johnson interrupted. "We have an urgent matter to attend to, but Ms. Boudreaux, I would like to ask you a few questions later."

"OK," Melody answered.

That said, Johnson bounced with the other three detectives on his heels. Explaining the phone conversation to them, he told Boston and Jimenez to meet a dive squad at the San Leandro Marina while he and Hernandez provided backup for Foster and McDavid on their undercover assignment.

Five minutes later, they rolled up to the back of the Parkside Terrace, where Foster, McDavid, and three uniformed San Leandro cops waited. After introductions,

Hernandez joined two of the officers and headed to the front of the building.

Foster and McDavid would remain in their ride so as not to blow their cover; if all three suspects came out, the job of arresting them would fall on Johnson and the lone patrol cop. Johnson issued instructions to the beat cop, along with Foster and McDavid. With the game plan set, everyone went to their assigned positions. The moment each man assumed his post, Leroy and Rodney walked out the gate drinking from red plastic cups. Johnson informed Hernandez by transmitter that Big Ed was still inside.

Back at Highland, Dr. Guillory and Guadalupe were called to duty, leaving Horace, Crystal, and Peaches (who'd convinced Lupe to let her hang with her friend) with Melody. Leaning over her bed while whispering directly into her ear, Horace began his personal interrogation.

"Peanut, can you tell me what happened?"

"OK brother, but promise you won't do nothing stupid."

"I promise." Horace crossed his fingers behind his back.

"Crystal's new man Big Ed ain't shit," she said. "He killed Silky."

"How do you know that?"

"Everybody knows 'cept Crystal, right Peaches?"

Peaches nodded her head in agreement while Crystal tensed up. Opening her mouth to speak, she was silenced by a wave of Horace's hand.

"Who did this to you?" he pressed on.

"Junebug."

"Junebug?" asked Peaches, whose voice rose four octaves.

"Shut up, gurl, and let her finish."

The deep baritone voice in which Horace spoke to Peaches, along with the deadly stare he gave her, let her know he meant business and she'd better keep quiet.

"Go on," he told his sister.

"See, we only wanted to break his ass."

"Break who?"

"Big Ed."

"What did you do?"

"I followed him to his mother's house in Hayward and watched him come out of the garage with what I knew had to be cash, drugs, or both."

"Then?"

"I went to Crystal's and saw Junebug drive up in her car because Big Ed and his brother had been arrested."

Horace thought for a minute about what he'd just heard, then resumed his fact-finding session. It didn't make sense but he was determined to get to the bottom of it.

"What happened then?" he coaxed.

"Big Ed left his keys in the cup holder so I took them from Junebug."

"You took them?" Horace asked with doubt.

"Well, he gave them to me ... reluctantly," she sighed before continuing. "Next, we went back to his parents' home and I searched the garage."

"You said 'I'—where was Junebug?"

"That punk was still in the car!" Tears streamed down her face.

"Lil sis, you said you both wanted to break him. If that's true, then why did he remain in the car?"

"Junebug didn't want nothing to do with it. I guess I must have taken too long, because all of a sudden he came inside."

"And?" Horace was relentless.

"And we found his stash. He had guns, dope, and at least a quarter of a million dollars hidden behind a wall cabinet."

The amount she stated caused the room to become deadly silent. Even though she'd exaggerated the figure, they knew she must have found a very large amount of scrill.

"What did you do next?" Horace pressed on.

"We went to Don Castro Park. Once we got there, I started counting the money, but before I knew what was going on, Junebug started hitting me in the face."

Peanut began crying while Peaches felt a lump forming in her throat. Crystal sat dazed, feeling as if her world were crumbling right before her eyes. She just couldn't believe Big Ed had used her like a fool. Horace remained steadily focused, not flinching whatsoever.

"When did he shoot you?" Horace asked Peanut.

"I got out of the car and tried to run but fell down. Next thing I knew, I was here."

Horace sat stone-faced thinking to himself. The room was so quiet one could hear a pin drop. The next twenty minutes were spent with each person deep in their own thoughts.

After what seemed like an eternity, Horace kissed

Peanut on the cheek then gave Crystal a hug, along with reassuring her that everything would be alright. Nodding his head to Peaches, he walked out.

26
SMOOTH
GETAWAY

Big Ed spotted Hernandez and the two cops on the television monitor just as he was about to click off the remote. Thinking fast, he ordered his boys out of the unit. Before they reached the door leading to the back gate, he spoke.

"Yaw wait fo me outside—ah fa-got sumptin."

Turning on his heels, he went back in the direction of the condo as they walked out. Heading to the elevator instead, he pushed the call button and stepped inside when the door slid open. As soon as the door closed he heard footsteps running in the hallway. Using the key Crystal had given him, Big Ed inserted it, waiting impatiently as the elevator lumbered down to the underground parking garage.

Just as he stepped out, he heard a loud noise, which he knew to be the cops kicking the door in. The garage had security bars surrounding it on all four sides from street

level to the bottom of the first-floor units. This allowed Big
Ed a clear view of the chaos going on among Rodney,
Leroy, and the cops on the street.

What he saw chilled him to the bone, which was
unusual for Big Ed, who was reputed to have "ice in his
veins." Rodney was beating the shit out of a police officer
while Leroy squatted between two cars in a stand-off with
Five-O, gun at the ready.

Badly as he wanted to, he couldn't wait around to see
what transpired. Leroy and Rodney were on their own; so
was he, for that matter. Crouching down low, Big Ed ran
the distance of the garage in the opposite direction and
out a side door that led to a public parking lot. Walking
across the street hurriedly, he got into his Benz and drove
off. Once he passed all the speeding police cars heading
towards the Parkside Terrace, he let out a huge sigh. Using
the speed-dial feature on his cell phone, he called Robin.

"Hello," she greeted.

"Baby, listen up closely—it's impotant."

"OK."

"Get dressed and meet me at the mall in front of
Mickey Dee's. Brang da money, but leave da dope an guns
at yo pad."

"What time?"

"Right now." He gritted his teeth.

"I'm on my way."

Robin hung up the phone and slipped on a pair of hip-
hugging jeans along with zipping up a blue sweatjacket.
Pulling a do-rag from her dome, she did a once-over in
the mirror to make sure her finger-waved perm was tight.

Satisfied, she slipped on a pair of sneakers and hoisted the duffel bag onto the sofa. Hurrying to the back room, she returned with a black travel bag that she stuffed full of cash. Jumping in her Seville, she rolled to the mall.

Big Ed drove down San Leandro Boulevard obeying all speed limits. Fast as his heart was racing, he knew that one infraction resulting in a traffic stop would definitely lead to his arrest. Passing motorists leered at him evilly as they went around because he was slowing up the flow of traffic.

Taking 74th to Hegenberger, he turtled to the mall. Robin was already there, waiting patiently. Big Ed pulled alongside then joined her in her ride. Robin leaned over and kissed him on the mouth.

"You look like you saw a ghost," she said.

"Da pigs got Leroy and Rod."

"For real?" She showed surprise.

"Yeah—dey woulda got me too but ah saw 'em first."

"What are you gonna do?"

"Ah gotta skip town, so ah need you to take me to the airport."

Her heart fell. "May I ask where you're going?"

"Ah'm goin ta Vegas, kick it wit mah folks for a while."

"Does this mean I won't see you anymore?"

Big Ed noticed the tears falling freely down Robin's face, which caused a pang of guilt to overcome him. Lifting up her chin, he looked her directly in the eye.

"Of course you'll see me." He sounded convincing. "Once I get settled in, ah'll send for you then we can be together, okay?"

"Okay." This news made her smile because now she would finally have her man all to herself.

"Now here's the plan. Take the dope an give it to Mugsy and Damon to sell. They'll give you half of the profit, and the rest they keep."

"You don't want any?"

"Naw, ah got enuff scrillah ta last me for years. You save what you get so when you come to live with me we'll have bookoo bank."

"What about the guns?" she asked.

"Sell 'em to the highest bidder," Bid Ed stated emphatically.

"How will I be able to reach you?"

"You won't—ah'll call you."

"Honey, I'm scared."

"Look baby, ah needs you ta be dare fo me—ah can trust you, right?"

"You know that," she answered.

"Good, now drive me to the airport."

"What about your car?" she asked while starting the engine.

"You keep it."

Robin drove to the airport in silence. Things were happening much too fast for her to digest. She only kept her composure by dreaming of a life with Big Ed. Pulling into the terminal, she wheeled her Caddy up to Southwest's passenger drop-off zone.

Big Ed kissed her hungrily before hopping out and joining the throng of travelers heading to all parts of the globe. Standing in the ticket line with his travel bag strapped across his shoulder, his senses were on full alert.

Since his plane wouldn't depart for another forty-five minutes, Big Ed checked in at Gate 12 then made a bee-line to the restroom, where he would remain until board-ing. Pulling out his cell phone, he called Muggsy, then Damon, informing them of the situation. He also gave them the names and numbers of all his contacts before anointing those two joint kingpins. Calling Shirley's house, he asked to speak to his children, which she denied. Next he called his mother, telling her he loved her but would be going away for a while. He didn't tell her about Leroy because he knew it would upset her, and once booked, Leroy would be calling collect anyway begging for money and care boxes.

As passengers began boarding the plane, Big Ed, who'd been watching all activity from the confines of the rest-room door, tossed his cell phone in the trash then got in line.

Comfortably seated, he closed his eyes as the plane shot down the runway.

Once airborne, he thought about the life he was leaving and the new life he would have to make. Now he could finally live a crime-free existence where no one knew of him or his reputation.

27
TWO DOWN, ONE TO GO

Boston and Jimenez entered the homicide office, marching directly to Johnson and Hernandez's cubicle. They'd waited for the dive squad to arrive at the marina, and after prying the latches open on the retrieved trunk, tore away the plastic bag. Finding the gun along with Junebug's very dead corpse, they knew Big Ed and his henchmen would be spending the rest of their natural lives in jail.

"Good news Sarge, if that's an appropriate way to put it," Boston said to Johnson.

"You got the chest?" Johnson asked.

"Yes, the divers retrieved it," Maria answered.

"What did you find?"

"We found a gun along with a dead body. Get this—the guy had gunshot residue on his fingers."

"Was he shot?"

"Negative, the victim died from asphyxiation. Not only

was he placed inside a trash bag in the chest, but his wrists, ankles, and breathing passages were duct-taped tighter than a drum."

"A horrible way to go," winced Hernandez. "You got a name?"

"Yes sir," answered Boston. "Anthony Grimes."

"That's him!" Johnson screamed, snapping his fingers in the process. "I knew he looked familiar but just couldn't place the guy."

"You know him?" Maria asked.

"We met once—he used to hang out with Silky Johnson. I guess that old saying is true."

"What old saying is that, sir?"

"Birds of a feather flock together."

"How does that tie in to this?" Maria didn't comprehend.

"They're both dead," Johnson answered matter-of-factly.

"Well," Boston broke the silence that had overcome the office, "once we get the lab results from the gun, I'm sure all loose ends will come together."

"What's up with that?" questioned Hernandez.

"The crime lab is tracing the gun as we speak."

As the words left Maria's mouth, Jimmy Chang entered the office. The gun dangled from his free hand in a zip-lock evidence bag that had been tagged and labeled.

Wah Woon Chang was his given name, but like most foreigners he adopted a more American one, Jimmy. Chang was the number-one evidence tech due to his meticulous approach and attention to even the slightest detail. Jet-black hair along with an upside-down pyramid-shaped head, the dude was sharp as a tack.

"What you got, Jimmy?" Johnson asked as Chang exchanged handshakes with everyone.

"Boss, gun is one used to shoot girl."

"Boudreaux?" Johnson asked.

"Correct, dumb criminals, shoot girl then hide gun in chest!" Jimmy gave off that familiar high-pitched laugh.

"Hold on," Johnson stated, "what about the residue on Grimes' hands?"

"He shoot girl," Jimmy deadpanned.

"So what we have here is Grimes shoots Melody, but doesn't kill her. Then, Tatum and his flunkeys kill Grimes and not only throw away the body, but the gun too."

"Correct boss," Jimmy co-signed.

"Let's put all the pieces in place," Johnson began. "For some unknown reason, Grimes attempts to kill Boudreaux, then drives her car to Sunnyside, where he's spotted by Foster and McDavid."

"—who follow them to the dump-off spot," Hernandez cut in.

"Arroyo Park," chimed Maria.

"While they're doing that, Tatum kills Grimes?" questioned Boston.

"Absolutely," affirmed Johnson. "Next, they dump the chest containing Grimes and the weapon in the marina."

"...then are followed to Melody's sister Crystal's home, where we nab 'em," said Hernandez.

"Two of 'em," corrected Nathan.

"Well, those two will be spending a very long time on vacation," commented Boston.

"And once we locate Big Ed, so will he," stated Maria.

"Here's the plan, guys," Johnson boomed. "We check airports, bus and train stations, along with rental car agencies."

"For Tatum?" asked Hernandez.

"Yes."

"We're on it, Sarge," Boston volunteered.

"Jimmy"—Johnson extended his hand—"good work."

"Thanx boss." Chang shook it.

Jimmy walked out smiling, with the zip-lock bag still dangling from his hand. He loved his job and the fact that Johnson truly appreciated the fine work he did. Boston and Jimenez went to their assigned desks and began placing phone calls to transportation agencies throughout the city. Johnson and Hernandez began writing their reports on Rodney and Leroy. Now they had no need to interview those two clowns because the evidence against them was overwhelming. They would be spending the rest of their lives in jail.

Once the reports were complete, the two detectives headed home.

28
PEANUT'S REVENGE

"Yeah baby," Big Ed told Robin, "I have a place waiting for you—your new home."

"Honey, these have been the loneliest three months of my life. I can't wait to see you."

"I feel the same, gurlll, just don't miss your flight."

"Hey, I'll be there and on time."

"An ah'll be waitin."

Big Ed hung up the phone and headed for the casinos. During the three-month manhunt he'd changed his appearance dramatically. He now possessed a full-grown beard, mustache, and goatee along with dreadlocks that nearly reached his shoulders.

Spending his days making parley bets on football and basketball, he was actually turning a profit. He'd convinced his cousin Naomi to purchase a home for him in her name for a twenty-thousand-dollar fee. A nice three-bedroom tract home that would demand a two-hundred-thousand-dollar asking price in the Bay Area, they got for one-ten in Vegas. Big Ed had the home fully furnished and knew his only difficult assignment would be to co-exist with Robin's kids.

Robin returned the receiver to its holder, cradling the phone against her chest. She would now have the only man she ever truly loved to herself. Set with more than one hundred grand, she packed up her most sentimental belongings, gathered up her three children, and called a cab.

Exiting the taxi at the airport, she rewarded the driver with a hundred-dollar tip. When the plane landed, Robin and her children went to the conveyor belt to wait for their luggage. Informing the cab driver of her new address, she rode to the destination on cloud nine.

Big Ed greeted them at the front door with a broad smile on his face. Robin was amazed at his visual transformation.

"Welcome home, baby!" he said.

"Look at you—Big Ed Tatum? Or do I have the wrong house?"

"You got the right house, and yes, it's me," he grinned. "Now give me a hug!"

"Ooh baby, it's so good to see you!"

"It's good to see you too. Do you like the your new home?"

"Yes, I love it, but I'll have to get used to the way you look."

"I'm glad you like it 'cause it's all yours. Let me take

you on a tour."

Leading the way, Big Ed showed them the bedrooms, kitchen, living and dining quarters, family room, and back yard, where the children squealed with glee at the sparkling new swimming pool.

Robin thought she was dreaming. Never in her wildest imagination would she have pictured something as beautiful as this to be her home.

"Honey, I'm speechless."

"Don't be baby—it's all real," said Big Ed.

"I can't believe we're in Vegas. When will we see the Strip?"

"In time, baby, in time."

Robin leaned on her toes and gave Big Ed a very sensuous kiss. Big Ed felt his manhood stirring, causing him to pull her closer. Being the sex maniac she was, she asked, "Do you want me to have the kids fix up their room so we can make love?"

She wanted nothing better than to have Big Ed's meat planted deep inside her. However, he had other ideas.

"I'll tell you what," he said, "you get everybody situated, let me go check on my bets, then we'll make love tonight and tour the Strip tomorrow. OK?"

"Alright," she answered.

Robin trailed Big Ed through the kitchen past the laundry room. When he opened up the back door leading to the garage, she screamed.

"The small one's yours," Big Ed grinned.

"Baby, I love you!"

Big Ed got into the larger Mercedes and backed out of

the driveway. As the garage door slowly closed, he smiled because Robin stood in a trance gazing at her "smaller" Benz.

Casino action was light due to the fact that most of the hardcore gamblers and big-money players usually arrived in the late evening. The place was sparsely populated with tourists and nickel slot players hoping for a miracle return from the one-armed bandits.

Big Ed strutted through the gaming area to the sports & race book, where as usual he was greeted by a crowded area of bettors laying down heavy dough on golf, boxing, football, and hoops. Since he had become a familiar sight to the guards and staff, no one even considered the large black man in dreads a threat—much less one of America's most wanted.

Carefully checking his tickets, Big Ed realized he had some winners amongst his stack. Grinning broadly while heading to the cashier's booth, he patiently waited in the short winners' line to collect.

He'd wagered three hundred, all twenty-dollar bets on five team parley cards, which would pay five-hundred-dollar returns for each winning ducat. With three hits amongst his fifteen tickets, he would make fifteen hundred, resulting in a twelve-hundred-dollar profit for a day's work.

"Good day, Mohammed?" asked Jerome the cashier.

"The usual, J-Dog," answered Big Ed. Mohammed was the alias he'd been using since arriving in Vegas.

Jerome was a nerdish-looking white dude who was

short, fat, and as lame as they came. He loved it when
Mohammed cashed out at his window because the dude
always left a fifty-dollar tip. He also enjoyed being referred
to as "J-Dog" since that title gave his insecure ass a feeling of being hip.

"Let's see what we got here," said Jerome as he scanned
the tickets. "Man-oh-man, fifteen duckaroos."

"Good deal, huh?" Big Ed asked.

"Mohammed, I don't know how you do it."

"It's called mathematics, homes—see you tomorrow."

Big Ed handed Jerome his tip, then walked out of the
race book area past the main casino. Walking through the
parking lot, he noticed from a distance that one of his
tires was flat as a pancake.

"Damn!" he shouted to no one in particular. Taking
off his jacket, he opened the trunk, tossed it inside, then
began searching for the spare.

Automobiles came and went with Big Ed paying them
no mind as he replaced the flat tire with a donut replace-
ment. A dark blue mid-sized sedan pulled into the stall
next to him, and an elderly gentleman began slowly getting out.

Glancing over his shoulder briefly, Big Ed continued
the task at hand. Suddenly he felt a gloved hand cover his
mouth, a knee press on his back, and the cold steel of a
knife blade slash his throat.

Big Ed struggled to breathe and attempted to stop the
flow of blood by covering his neck with his hands. Feeling his body being dragged to the front of the car, he looked
up at the perpetrator, attempting to speak.

"Sweetpea...," he whispered as blood gushed from his neck.

"Die a slow death, motherfucker."

Sweetpea hopped into his rental car and drove away as Big Ed felt life leave his body. His dead corpse would not be discovered for three hours.

Taking the car back to the rental agency, Sweetpea boarded the next flight to Oaktown. Once there, he went to the restroom, where he discarded his fake mustache, sideburns, goatee, and afro wig.

Re-emerging with a totally different appearance, he exited the terminal and headed for Highland General to visit his sister Peanut. Also to resume his bland lifestyle as Horace Boudreaux. That is, until his next kill.

BACK TO NORMAL

Robin sat propped up in bed stark naked reading a magazine. She wondered where her man was but didn't trip on it because all she could think of was feeling his penis deep inside her body.

The newscaster on the tube was describing a grisly murder scene in the parking lot of one of the major casinos. Robin recognized the car and the body, which the newsman described as a mystery person.

Crying softly, she rose up and began re-packing clothes into her suitcase. Gathering up her children along with her bundle of cash, she lifted the keys to her Mercedes from the kitchen counter and drove back to Oaktown.

The nine-hour drive was of no concern because she wasn't going to give back the car. Since her man was dead and Five-O didn't know who he was, she would keep the car for her trouble.

Now she was glad she had not told her landlord she was moving. Pulling into the driveway of her apartment complex on Sunnyside, she vowed never again to fall in love with a drug dealer.

That self-made promise only lasted two weeks because before Valentine's Day, Robin McGee was in love with yet another d-boy.

NEW NUMBER ONE

Johnson sat in the courtroom smiling. Leroy and Rodney were convicted for the murder of Anthony "Junebug" Grimes. They were also charged with attempted murder of Silky Johnson but that didn't stick.

Happy as they were, Johnson and his partner Hernandez still yearned for the capture of Big Ed Tatum. Returning to the office, they received an e-mail bulletin from Las Vegas Metro informing them that Big Ed Tatum had been murdered.

He'd been using the alias Mohammed Abdul Shariff, but fingerprints and dental charts provided a positive ID. It was Tatum, without a doubt.

"Let's go get lunch," said Hernandez.

"I'm right behind you," Johnson answered.

Taking the one-block trek to the Rose, Johnson ordered

a steak burrito plate while Hernandez requested a crab enchilada dinner.

"So we have a new member to the exclusive club, huh?" Hernandez asked while munching on salsa and chips.

"Looks that way," Johnson deadpanned.

They spent the next ten minutes waiting for their food while discussing the newest unknown member on Oaktown's most-wanted list. They agreed to create a criminal profile on the guy and spend all their extra time searching for leads.

The waitress placed their grub on the table, which they began eating like the starving detectives they were. Even though each man was absorbed deep in his own thoughts and had hundreds of questions and theories, as usual, they ate in silence.

Questions or comments, email Renay:
LADAYPUBLISHING@CS.COM
Thanks for your support!!

ABOUT THE AUTHOR

Renay Jackson is a former rapper and the self-proclaimed godfather of urban lit. *Peanut's Revenge* is the fourth and final novel in his Oaktown Mystery Series, which began with *Oaktown Devil, Shakey's Loose,* and *Turf War,* all published by Frog, Ltd. in 2004. Look for his fifth novel, *Crackhead,* in 2006.

Jackson received the Chester Himes Black Mystery Writer Award in 2002. When he's not writing or giving workshops, he spends his time tinkering with the bass guitar, solving cryptograms, and kicking it with his grandchildren. He resides in Oakland.